HYPERSPACE HIGH

THE SCHOOL THAT'S OUT OF THIS WORLD

Also in the

series:

CRASH LANDING

FROZEN ENEMIES

ROBOT WARRIORS

GALACTIC BATTLE

SPACE PLAGUE

HYPERSPACE HIGH

WARLORD'S REVENGE

ZAC HARRISON

First published in 2013 by Curious Fox,
an imprint of Capstone Global Library Limited,
7 Pilgrim Street, London, EC4V 6LB
Registered company number: 6695582

www.curious-fox.com

Text © Hothouse Fiction Ltd 2013

Series created by Hothouse Fiction
www.hothousefiction.com

The author's moral rights are hereby asserted.

Cover Illustration by Dani Geremia

ISBN 978 1 78202 003 5

1 3 5 7 9 10 8 6 4 2

A CIP catalogue for this book is available from the British Library.

Typeset in Avenir by Hothouse Fiction Ltd

Printed and bound in the United Kingdom by CPI

MIX
Paper from
responsible sources
FSC
www.fsc.org
FSC® C020471

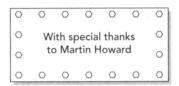

With special thanks
to Martin Howard

CHAPTER 1

John Riley reeled backwards, as a heavy punch smashed into his face. He slammed into the side of the fight cage, causing the metal fence to rattle. Rising to his feet with difficulty, he grimaced at his opponent. "Nice move, Kaal," he said. He checked himself over. His armour was battered and torn; one arm hung useless by his side. His power was down to ten per cent, and his health was used up.

The fight was going badly.

The crowd roared, crying out for more. John looked up at the flashing scoreboard. Kaal was leading by eight points, with less than fifteen seconds until the end of the match. John needed a knockout to win. Staggering, he launched himself at his best friend, his remaining fist pulled back for a massive blow.

Kaal's great leathery wings snapped out. "Come on, then, tiny Earthling!" he yelled. His wings beat the air, and he flew to the top of the cage.

John's fist met nothing but empty air. Nervously, he looked up. The diving attack was one of Kaal's favourites. It was totally devastating.

If he catches me …

As the green alien dropped, face grinning in demonic glee, John kicked away from the ground. With a shout of "Anti-grav!" he soared into the air, spinning. An unexpected mid-air roundhouse kick crunched into Kaal's chest.

"Ooof!" grunted the Derrilian, falling backwards.

John crashed into the fight cage, using it to kick off back towards Kaal. "Power strike!" he yelled. An armoured fist, blazing white light, crunched into his friend's jaw, throwing him back. "*Gotcha!*" John yelled, laughing. "Crushed like a bug, Riley-styley."

Wings hanging limp, Kaal slid down the bars, landing in a heap on the floor.

"KNOCKOUT!" a huge voice bellowed. "JOHN RILEY WINS WITH THREE SECONDS TO SPARE!"

Around the cage, thousands of aliens rose from their seats and cheered their approval. Tentacles, hands, claws, and flippers slapped together; shouts of "JOHN! JOHN!" filled the air. Lights flashed. John put one foot on the slumped body of his friend, as a ring of stars and planets spun around Kaal's head. Roaring in triumph, he raised a glowing fist in triumph.

"Oh for the love of Sillar, you're going to be late for breakfast," said a girl's voice over the noise of the screaming crowd. "You're not even dressed yet."

Bowing to the vast audience of aliens, John sighed. "Quit Boxogle," he said. The fight cage and crowd disappeared in a blink, leaving only blackness before his eyes.

Reaching up, John pulled a close-fitting helmet off his head. "Morning, Emmie." He grinned at the beautiful golden-skinned girl leaning against the doorframe.

On the squashy black sofa opposite, Kaal removed his own helmet. He, too, grinned, revealing a mouth full of sharp white fangs. "Good fight," he said, leaning forwards to high-five John – an Earth custom that had caught on among John's friends. "That *almost* hurt. You were lucky, though. I'm going to totally pulverize you in the rematch ... Oh, hi Emmie. What time is it?"

By the door, Emmie Tarz hooked a mane of silvery hair behind a slightly pointed ear. She rolled her navy-blue eyes. "It's time for you to get out of virtual reality and into *reality* reality," she said. "I can't believe you're playing Boxogle at this time of the morning. Class starts in less than half an hour and you're still in your pyjamas."

"Don't bother telling them," said a voice that seemed to come from nowhere. "I have been saying they need to get ready the last twenty minutes. It's quite useless." Zepp, the ship's computer, sounded almost as exasperated as Emmie.

"Thirty minutes? If we skip breakfast, there's still plenty of time," said Kaal, leaning back. "Want a quick game, Emmie?"

Emmie snorted. "You want your butt kicked twice in one morning, do you?"

"I must remind you that breakfast is the most important meal of the day, and in addition, the

Examiners punish lateness with detention," Zepp said.

"OK, OK," said John, jumping up. Hauling a silver and red Hyperspace High jumpsuit out of his locker, he looked over his shoulder. "Come on, Kaal. Unless you'd rather sit in detention than face me in a rematch later."

"You wish," said Kaal, reaching for his own jumpsuit as John headed into the bathroom.

"Please hurry up. I'm *starving*," Emmie muttered.

A few minutes later the three students were running along a corridor towards the canteen. "There are more important things in life than virtual reality games, you know," Emmie said, panting.

"There are?" John shot back. "Like what?"

"She's talking some sort of crazy gibberish," Kaal said, grinning. "There's *nothing* more important than virtual reality games ... Hey, what on Derril is *that*?" Kaal skidded to a halt so quickly that John ran into his back.

"Hey, watch where ..." John's annoyance trailed off as he also found himself glancing out the viewing window.

"Wow!" gasped Emmie, jogging to a halt beside

him. "That's incredible."

John took a step closer to the window. Outlined by stars, an enormous pyramid of shining purple cruised alongside Hyperspace High. Its smooth sides gleamed, looking as if they were made of glass lit from within. Nothing broke the flawless expanse of purple – no sign of engines or any markings. Mysterious and beautiful, the huge pyramid slipped through space, closer and closer to one of the gigantic white wings that housed Hyperspace High's sensors, force field generators, and hangar decks. The pyramid, however, was far too large to fit inside even Hyperspace High's cavernous hangars. As John watched, the craft swung to a docking port.

A faint shudder ran through the deck beneath John's feet, as the pyramid was joined to the great bulk of Hyperspace High by the huge docking clamps.

"Whoa," John said under his breath. "Every time I think I'm getting used to weird space stuff, something even more freaky comes along."

He had been at the space school for only half a term. Seven weeks ago one of the teachers had mistaken him for a Martian prince. He had been brought on board by accident – and then nearly thrown out of an airlock into space. The headmaster had stepped in at the last moment, giving him a temporary place as a student. The place had become permanent after John helped his classmates escape an exploding volcano planet.

Since then, while John's parents believed he was at a boarding school in Derbyshire, he had fought warrior aliens, flown spaceships at faster-than-light speed, learned to use technologies far beyond anything on Earth, and met bizarre beings from hundreds of different worlds. He had even eaten in a restaurant that only served eyeballs. Strange things had become so commonplace that John often thought he'd be shocked if he weren't freaked out at least once a day.

But even with all of this, the pyramid was breathtaking.

"Is that a *spaceship*?" John asked, realizing it was a ridiculous question even as he said it. *Of course it's a spaceship, idiot,* he told himself. *You can tell by the way it flies through space.*

If it was a stupid question, however, neither of his friends seemed to notice.

"It must be," breathed Emmie, as they hurried to the canteen. "But I've never seen anything like it before, or even *heard* of a ship like it. And I thought I knew every model in the universe."

"We'd better eat fast," said Kaal, as he pulled a tray from the dispenser in the table. "Hmm, flavworms. I was hoping for klatfingers."

John glanced over Kaal's shoulder as he sat, realizing it was a mistake as soon as he saw the bowl of writhing pink worms. Wrinkling his nose, he tried to ignore Kaal taking his first mouthful and pulled his own tray closer.

"Ugh, you've got those horrible bird bottom things *again*," said Emmie in disgust.

"Eggs. They're called eggs. And they're a lot nicer than … than … whatever that disgusting gloop is you're eating."

"It's Sillaran slurrige," replied Emmie. "Very tasty and full of healthy goodness. Here, try some." She held out a spoon overflowing with lumpy goo towards John.

John rocked back in his chair. "I'll stick with the eggs, thanks."

"So where do you think that ship came from?" asked Kaal, through a mouthful of worms. "Do you think we're being raided by space pirates?"

"Don't be ridiculous, Kaal," replied Emmie. "It's an amazing ship, though. I hope it's a new model and Jegger's going to let us fly it."

"It's a lot bigger than a t-dart or a Xi-Class Privateer," said John doubtfully. The spaceships he'd flown for Space Flight class were tiny compared to the huge pyramid.

"That's why it would be so much fun," said Emmie, waving her spoon about. "Imagine how much power a ship that size must have." Her eyes glistened with excitement – Emmie was one of Hyperspace High's top pilots and loved nothing more than trying out a new ship. "Imagine how *fast* it could go," she finished.

"Imagine trying to *land* it," John replied. "It's difficult enough in a t-dart."

"Maybe we've picked it up because it's in distress," Kaal said thoughtfully. "Engine failure or something."

"Could be visitors from another universe," John suggested, putting on a spooky voice. "Aliens from other worlds." He meant it as a joke and was surprised to see Emmie and Kaal both nod their heads.

"Could be," said Emmie. "My dad says the Galactic Fleet occasionally gets reports of unidentified flying objects. Some people think they might be ships from parallel universes or galaxies on the other side of black holes."

Kaal nodded. "There are millions of planets with life on them we haven't discovered yet."

John almost choked on a piece of toast. "You mean UFOs?" he gasped. He stared at his friends: Kaal who looked like a huge, green demon, and Emmie with her softly glowing skin and pointy ears. "*You* believe in aliens?"

Emmie stared at him. "What's so funny about that?"

"On my planet, Hyperspace High would be a UFO. *You* would be aliens. I'm talking to aliens who believe in aliens!"

Kaal patted him on the shoulder. "Yes, but your planet is a bit … umm … how can I put this?"

"Backwards," said Emmie with a grin.

"Undeveloped, I was going to say." Kaal patted John's shoulder again. "But don't worry, it should catch up in another ten thousand years or so."

John couldn't help laughing. Everyone on the ship, except the headmaster, seemed to think that the people of Earth were primitive, but he knew his friends were only teasing him. He was about to retort, when a chime rang through the canteen.

"Uh oh," said Kaal quickly, shovelling in the last mouthful of flavworms. "Better get going."

The pyramid ship forgotten, John jumped to his feet and snatched the bag that contained his ThinScreen. "What have we got this morning anyway? I've completely forgotten."

"Space Survival," said Emmie, as they hurried down a corridor. "And we've got five minutes to get there or we'll all be in detention."

As they started running to class, a pulsing ball of bright light zipped past, headed in the direction of the docking port. For a second it continued on its way before coming to a sudden stop and heading back towards them.

In a flash, the bright light changed into the shape of a bald alien wearing robes as white as snow. His skin shimmered softly, and his purple eyes twinkled with energy.

"Good morning, sir," Kaal, Emmie, and John chorused together.

Lorem, the headmaster of Hyperspace High, raised an eyebrow. Usually, he enjoyed stopping and chatting with students he met along the ship's passages, taking time to find out how their studies were going and swapping jokes. Today, however, he seemed to be in a rush. "The three of you are late for class," he said, without wishing them a good morning.

"Errr … yeah," John spluttered. "We were just—"

"Playing Boxogle?" Lorem finished for him.

There was a moment of silence. "*Well?*" the headmaster said, raising his eyebrow again.

"Yes, sir." John knew it would be no use making up another excuse – not when the headmaster could see things that were hidden from most people. Sometimes even the future.

"Tomorrow morning you may wish to spend less time playing Boxogle and more time brushing your hair."

With a wink of his purple eye, Lorem vanished in a flash of light. John ran to catch up with his friends, running fingers through his untidy mop of blond hair, as they watched the ball of energy disappear in the distance.

Freaky space stuff, John thought again.

CHAPTER 2

John, Emmie, and Kaal bundled into the holo-classroom with seconds to spare. Around an open hill side, a forest of pink and orange trees stretched far into the distance. Winged lizard-like creatures chattered in a light yellow sky with two suns. At the front of the class, the teacher was taking a seat on an old tree stump.

The three students found themselves smaller stumps. In the blue grass at John's feet was a QuickFan, a small propeller on a simple harness. Controlled with a hand-held joystick the size of a pencil, the QuickFan was used to fly in zero-gravity. John eyed it curiously, wondering what sort of lesson Professor Raydon, the Space Survival teacher, had in store.

A native of planet Arborill, Raydon looked half-man, half-tree. Tall and slim with knotted, bark-like skin, the professor had long hair that was autumn gold. He wore a simple tunic and trousers, while tools hung from a leather belt around his waist. Black eyes under heavy brows looked over the class, checking that none of the students was missing. At his feet, a fire crackled merrily.

"Good morning," said Raydon when he had finished his class count. His voice sounded like a tree creaking. He pointed down at the flames at his feet. "Fire," he anounced. "It can be your best friend, or it can kill you. Last week, we covered lighting fires in inhospitable conditions, but can anyone tell me how best to put one out?"

Before anyone else could speak, a boy with two long, black tentacles sprouting from his ribcage snapped one in the air. "Deprive the fire of its oxygen source!" he blurted out quickly.

A small metal ball floating by his shoulder whispered, "Oh, *very* good, sir," in its robotic voice.

Mordant Talliver's Serve-U-Droid, G-Vez, stretched out a thin silver arm and brushed a crease from its master's red and silver jumpsuit.

John frowned. He himself had known the answer, but Mordant liked to remind everyone how clever he was. The black-haired half-Gargon always tried to answer any questions before anyone else could get a word in.

"Yes, Mordant Talliver is correct," creaked Professor Raydon. He put his head to one side, staring at Mordant. "A little rude not waiting to be called on, but correct all the same. Can anyone think of another way to put out fire? Emmie Tarz, how about you?"

"Ummm …" said Emmie. "That is … ahhh …"

John glanced round at her. Emmie was biting her bottom lip, a sure sign that she was flustered and nervous. *Come on, Emmie*, he thought, silently urging her to answer. *It's really obvious.* He knew Emmie hated the fact that she was close to the bottom in almost every class, and he also knew she worked hard to improve her marks. In fact, she had been up late last night, cramming her Cosmic Languages coursework.

Mordant Talliver broke the silence. "Ha," he

sniggered quietly. "Emmie Tarz, the universe's biggest idiot, strikes again." In a louder voice, he continued, "Sir, the answer is—"

"Water!" John blurted, interrupting him. "On Earth we put out fires with water."

"That's right. Thank you, John; though I wasn't asking you *or* Mordant." With long, twig-like fingers, Raydon picked up a water bottle at his feet and tipped it onto the little fire. It steamed and fizzled out. "The water displaces oxygen and turns to steam," he said. "Which moves heat away from the fire. It's a very effective way of putting out most fires, used across the universe. *If* you are in normal gravity." He paused for a moment. "But we're in space, and in an emergency the gravity might fail. What happens then?"

The class was silent.

"Nothing to say, Talliver or Riley? Stumped you, have I, eh? Well, let's try it, shall we?" Raydon stood up. "Please strap on your QuickFans. Zepp, give me zero-gravity and cancel the holo program."

"Certainly, Professor Raydon," Zepp replied, as John pulled the QuickFan harness over his shoulders and buckled it at his chest.

The hill and forest vanished. The class now stood in a large domed room, covered with what looked like small white studs. These were the hologram projectors that could create any environment imaginable . Feeling a lightness in his stomach as the gravity was turned off, John flicked the switch on his QuickFan, thanking his stars that Kaal had taught him how to use one – for once, he wasn't going to embarrass himself by thrashing around like a drowning cat in zero-gravity. Buzzing blades whirred as the machine on his back came to life. John's feet left the ground as the small propeller shot him towards the ceiling. He cut the power after a second and floated to a stop a few metres above the floor. Around him the rest of the class did the same, seventeen students from seventeen different worlds hanging in a circle in mid-air.

In the centre, Professor Raydon pulled a small white sphere from a leather pouch at his hip. Clicking a small device, he set fire to it and let go as the flames caught.

John stared. A ball of fire, about the size of a football, spun in the air, its surface boiling gold, red, and white. It looked beautiful. *Like a tiny sun*, he thought.

"Who would like to try and extinguish the flame?"

Once again, Mordant's tentacle shot up. Raydon ignored it. Angling his own QuickFan so that he drifted away from the fireball, he said, "John, as you know so much about water, why don't you come here and try."

"Umm ... OK, sir." Carefully, John flew to the centre of the circle, stopping when he could feel the heat of the flames on his face.

"Here's your water," said the professor, tossing him a bottle.

John caught it, twisted off the lid, and squeezed it towards the fire. Water spurted out, forming a quivering bubble in zero-gravity. John watched as it wobbled towards the fireball, expecting it to put the fire out as soon as it touched the flame. Instead, the two balls – fire and water – met with a slight hiss and the fireball simply moved away, still burning brightly.

"Try again," Professor Raydon said.

This time, John squeezed the bottle harder, sending a gush of smaller bubbles towards the fireball. The result was exactly the same, though this time the ball moved away more quickly.

"Hey, don't send it in this direction, John," said Lishtig ar Steero. He hastily adjusted his QuickFan to move himself from the fireball's path, snatching his trailing ponytail of purple hair out of the way just in time.

"Sorry, Lishtig," John grinned. He chased the ball of flame through floating bubbles of water, lining up for a third shot.

"Allow me to put it out for you," the teacher said, flying over and taking the bottle from his hand.

To John's amazement, instead of squirting it at the fire, Raydon tucked the water bottle into his pocket. Empty-handed, he twisted in the air until he was facing the fireball. "OUT!" he barked loudly.

The flames flickered and vanished.

"H-how on Earth, did you do that?" John stammered. Around him, the rest of the class looked on in stunned silence.

Professor Raydon spun slowly in the air, smiling at the class. "Without gravity, fire behaves very differently," he explained. "Although it is still possible to extinguish the flame with water, if you have the right equipment, for smaller fires it is much easier to use sound. Can anyone tell me why?" he looked around. "Yes, Kaal?"

Kaal lowered his hand. Sounding a little shy, he said, "I'm just guessing, but is it like blowing out the flame with a puff of air? Do the sonic waves scatter burning gases?"

"Exactly right, Kaal. I couldn't have put it better myself." Professor Raydon beamed. "In zero-gravity, a flame can be disrupted with sound waves, exactly as if you were blowing it out. This means that anyone who can shout loudly enough can put out a fire." Smiling, he continued. "So, let's see who can shout loudly enough."

Using his QuickFan expertly, Professor Raydon flew from one student to the next, lighting seventeen balls of flame and giving each of the students a few words of advice. "Yell, very quickly," he told John as he set a white ball ablaze. "You need a sudden burst of sound to disrupt the gas."

"OUT!" John bellowed a few moments later. In front of him, the fire sputtered, but soon became a steady ball of flame again, now drifting slowly across the room. The sound waves had only pushed it away.

He glanced around. Not one of his classmates had managed to extinguish their fireball on the first go. Now, they were all using their QuickFans to follow them around the huge dome. Fireballs were floating in every direction, and the classroom echoed with all sorts of loud sounds – from booming shouts to high-pitched shrieks.

"Be *careful*!" shouted Raydon. "If your fire is drifting too close to someone, make sure you warn them to get out of the way."

"Go OUT!" John shouted again, then "Rats," as the fireball just drifted a little further away again. Holding his QuickFan behind him, he gave the propeller a short burst of power and gave chase.

"Hurrah, *I did it*. Do I get a prize?" announced Gobi-san-Art in his deep, rumbling voice. John glanced round. The big craggy boy, who looked like he'd been carved from a great block of stone, was punching the air in triumph. His fireball had gone out.

"Well done, Gobi!" called Professor Raydon.

Turning back to his own fireball, John's eyes widened. It had drifted on and was now floating dangerously close to Mordant Talliver. "Hey, Mordant, watch out!" he shouted.

Too late.

Oh great, thought John, wincing as the flames brushed past the half-Gargon's elbow. *He's totally going to make a massive scene.*

Mordant's high-pitched squeal of pain instantly put out his own ball of flame.

"*Owwwww!*" he shrieked. "I'm burned. John *burned* me."

"Hey, I'm really sorry, I didn't mean to—"

"Yes, you did. G-Vez, you saw. He did it on purpose, didn't he?"

"The Earthling undoubtedly sent his fireball in your direction with every intention of harming you, young master Talliver," said G-Vez.

"That's not true," said John. "It was an accident. I was just looking the other way."

"I bet you were," spat Mordant, clutching his elbow. "Looking around to make sure Professor Raydon didn't see you burning me."

The professor swooped up between them. "What's going on here?" he demanded.

"John *burned* me, sir." Mordant showed the teacher

his elbow. He turned his head away as Raydon pushed up his sleeve. "Will I be permanently scarred?" he asked in a faint voice.

"Oh, I don't think so, Mister Talliver," Professor Raydon replied cheerfully. "These uniforms are flame-retardant. Look, the fire only singed the surface of the fabric. It hasn't even touched your skin. You're perfectly all right. And, if it makes you feel any better, you managed to put your fire out." Looking around, he dropped Mordant's elbow and shouted, "It's OK, everyone! Nothing to see here, get back to work."

As the shouting started again, Raydon frowned at John. "John, be a little more careful, please," he said before whirring away.

"But, sir, he did it on *purpose*!" Mordant shouted after him.

Once again, Raydon ignored him.

"It *was* an accident Mordant, and I *am* sorry," John said calmly. It had been plain on John's first day at Hyperspace High that he and Mordant Talliver were never going to be friends. Since then, John had saved the half-Gargon's life but, if anything, this seemed to have made the black-haired boy dislike him even more. Nevertheless, John didn't want to cause any more bad feelings between them.

"Yeah, *right*. Just don't think I'm going to forget this."

"The young master certainly does have an excellent memory," G-Vez agreed in its most self-important voice.

"Shut up, G-Vez. I'm not taking to you," snapped John.

"Don't tell my droid to shut up." One of Mordant's tentacles prodded John in the chest.

John slapped it away, his face reddening. "I'm trying to apologize, you stupid—"

A glow of light filled the room, as the headmaster zipped through the wall and flashed into his humanoid form. A door opened, and two Examiners floated into the room. Every student fell silent. Every student except Kaal, who was still intent on putting out his fire.

"AAAAAAARGH!" he screamed at his fireball.

CHAPTER 3

As Kaal's screech put out the flames , the Derrilian looked around in triumph. Spotting the headmaster, his face fell. "Oh, sorry, sir. I didn't see you there," Kaal mumbled.

"That's quite all right, Kaal," Lorem replied. "*Excellent* screaming, by the way. I shall certainly call on you if I need to extinguish a fire in zero-gravity."

While he was speaking, Examiners passed rapidly from student to student. Using force fields, the featureless white robots created spheres of green light around each of the remaining fireballs. Starved of oxygen, the flames died.

The headmaster turned to Raydon. "Professor, I'm sorry to disturb your class, but if you would be so kind …"

"Of course, headmaster," Raydon said, nodding. "Zepp," he said, "Restore gravity, please."

Zepp obeyed the teacher's request in an instant. Around the holo-classroom, students tumbled out of the air. John fell on his feet. Others weren't so lucky. A few students stood up, rubbing freshly bruised backsides.

"Ouch, Zepp. I nearly broke an ankle," Lishtig complained, wobbling to his feet.

"You should grow some wings," grinned Kaal, landing lightly and folding his own leathery wings across his back.

The headmaster raised a hand. "I have important news," he announced. His smile had faded. He looked, and sounded, extremely serious.

The students fell silent, eyes fixed on the headmaster. "Hyperspace High," the headmaster continued, "founded ten thousand years ago by the scholars of Kerallin …"

The students glanced at each other. This wasn't

news. Everyone knew the scholars of Kerallin had created the finest school in history as a gift to the universe.

But Lorem hadn't finished. "That much you all know," he continued. "What fewer people realize is that every 100 years, the scholars inspect one class of Hyperspace High students. Very few are chosen to study here, and standards at the school must remain high. The scholars want to make sure that every student is making good progress and to judge whether they deserve their places. Hyperspace High only teaches the very best, and it is not unknown for the scholars of Kerallin to ask students to leave if they are not reaching their full potential." Lorem paused for a moment, and then finished matter-of-factly. "This year, they will be testing you."

The news created an instant buzz. Around John, students began to chatter in excitement. The scholars of Kerallin were near-mythical figures who spent their lives wrapped in secret study on their hidden world. Very few beings in the universe had ever laid eyes upon them. Every so often the fruit of their research was presented by a messenger – new technology the scholars had invented, the histories of planets lost long ago, or works of mathematics so complex that that only a few minds in the universe could grasp their importance. Otherwise, the scholars stayed silent and apart from the rest of the universe.

"Wow," said Queelin Temerate, her yellow eyes glowing and stubby feelers twitching with excitement. "You mean the *actual* scholars are *actually* coming here?"

"And they're going to test us?" said Raytanna. "Oh goody, I just love tests."

A cold dread had gripped John's stomach. Although he tried his best, the only subjects he was any good at were maths and flying. As he had discovered when he first came to Hyperspace High, very few of the subjects taught at the school were anything like those he had been learning on Earth. John spent a lot of his time trying to catch up with the other students. A test on Galactic Geography or Hyperspace History was his worst nightmare. He gulped. What if the scholars wanted to test him on Cosmic Languages? Speaking alien languages was mind-bogglingly difficult for John, who had never even met an alien until seven weeks ago, let alone tried to communicate with one in their own language. He often thanked his lucky stars for the ship's computer, which translated every word that was spoken around him into English before it even reached his ears.

I'm going to fail.

He glanced at Emmie. Her golden skin had turned pale. She looked back at him, biting her lip. John knew exactly what she was thinking. Between the two of them, they juggled bottom place in most classes between them. One week it would be him, the next Emmie. There was every chance that both of them would fail a test.

Unlike Emmie, though, John had an extra worry. An accident had brought him to the school. Lorem had asked him to stay but he hadn't been specially chosen to study at Hyperspace High like everyone else. At least Emmie knew that the scholars must have had some reason for picking her. *Probably her talent at flying*, reflected John. *I don't want to be thrown out*, he told himself. *I'll have to go back to boring Earth school and never fly a spaceship again. Maybe if I study really hard before the test begins ...*

An Examiner interrupted his thoughts. Its flat, electronic voice droned, "Rule 109: Unauthorized speaking in class is prohibited. Future transgressions punishable by detention."

"I'm sure there will be no need for detentions," said the headmaster, as the class fell silent once more. "If I may continue … no, Queelin, the scholars will not be coming here. Many of them are too old to make the journey, so you will be travelling to Kerallin for the inspection. You will be representing the whole school, so I expect nothing less than your very best behaviour. Remember to apply *everything* you have learned at Hyperspace High."

He stopped again, looking from face to face. "There is one last thing," he said slowly. "I must warn you that the scholars are highly secretive. Once the test is finished, you must never speak of it to anyone. Do I make myself clear?"

A few students nodded.

"I will, of course, know if anyone is indiscreet," Lorem said, stony-faced.

"Yes, sir," the entire class chorused.

Before he knew what he was doing, John's hand

was up. "Excuse me, sir, but when does the test start? Will we have time to revise?"

"The tests begin *now*," Lorem answered. "The scholars are expecting you, and they wish to know what you have *learned*, not how well you revise."

John groaned inwardly.

"If you are all quite ready, then, let's get you on your way to Kerallin. Please follow me." Thanking Professor Raydon, Lorem turned and led the class from the holo-classroom.

In the corridor outside, the feverish chatter started again. "Wow, my mum and dad would never *believe* I've been to Kerallin," chuckled Lishtig. "It's, like, the brainiest place in the universe."

"Not if Emmie and John are there," sneered Mordant. "As soon as they land, it'll be the *thickest* place in the universe." Seeing John and Emmie's miserable faces, he added slyly, "What's the matter with you two? Afraid you're going to be thrown out? About time, if you ask me."

They both ignored him, too wrapped up in their own worries to argue.

"Get lost, Mordant," Kaal growled from behind them.

"I was just saying—"

"And I was just saying *get lost.*"

"Yeah? What are you going to do about it?"

"Maybe I'll call an Examiner over," snapped Kaal. "I'm sure they'll be very interested to know your idea of 'very best behaviour' involves insulting other students before we've even taken off."

Muttering under his breath, Mordant walked faster until he was out of earshot.

"Don't let Mordant bother you; he's an idiot," said Kaal gently.

"He's right, though," Emmie said glumly. "I'm never going to pass any tests."

"Me, neither," said John. "I'm going to let the school down and prove that Lorem never should have asked me to stay."

Clapping an enormous hand on each of his friends' shoulders, Kaal laughed. "Cheer up," he said. "The scholars of Kerallin would be mad to throw either of you out. Between you, you've saved everyone's lives on an exploding volcano planet, stopped an intergalactic war, and won the Robot Warrior competition."

"Yeah, but none of that involved *tests*,"John groaned.

"I might as well save myself a trip to Kerallin and start packing now," Emmie added glumly.

"Rubbish, you'll both be fine," said Kaal cheerfully. "Hey, you know where we're headed, don't you?"

John and Emmie stared at him. Neither of them had been paying any attention to where Lorem was leading the class.

"Where?" asked John.

"Exit port kappa," Kaal said, grinning.

It took a moment to work it out. Emmie got there first. "The pyramid!" she gasped, looking through a viewing window at the glowing ship that had docked with Hyperspace High earlier that morning. "We're going to Kerallin on that amazing spaceship." Her navy-eyes brightened immediately.

"I thought that might cheer you up," said Kaal.

A few minutes later, the headmaster brought the class to a halt outside the dock. "Here our paths must part," he told the students. "To ensure that none of you are coached or helped with the tests, the scholars forbid any teachers to accompany you.

Mordant Talliver, your Serve-U-Droid will also not be permitted."

Talliver gasped, "But ... but I *need* G-Vez. Without it, I'll have to do everything myself."

"That's the idea, Mordant."

"Serve-U-Droids are programmed to follow their owners everywhere," G-Vez cut in. "I would be failing in my duty if I allowed the young master to go without me."

"Think of it as a holiday," Lorem replied.

The little droid spun around, lights flashing. "Ah," it said, "if you put it that way, I have been meaning to change my batteries and tidy up my hard drive."

"G-VEZ!" Mordant sounded outraged.

For the first time since the headmaster had appeared in the classroom, John found himself smiling.

"I am terribly sorry, young Master Talliver," the little machine said, "But rules are rules." It floated away to bob around the headmaster's shoulders.

Lorem nodded towards the pyramid. "Your assessment begins now. Starting with tests of Space Flight and your problem-solving abilities."

"You mean we've got to fly the pyramid on our

own?" Emmie blurted out.

"Precisely. And pilot it to the Kerallin."

The last traces of Emmie's nerves vanished. "I didn't realize there would be a flight test," she said happily. "Space flight I can do."

"Well, now is your chance to show the scholars of Kerallin, " Lorem replied. Addressing the whole class, he continued, "Once you are all on board, we will release the docking clamps. The ship will be moved away from Hyperspace High using our force fields. After that, you are on your own. Whatever happens, I'm trusting all of you will make me proud. Good luck, everyone."

As the class filed through exit port kappa, a finger tapped John on the shoulder. He stopped and looked up into the headmaster's twinkling purple eyes.

"John Riley," Lorem said, "you look less than happy about this adventure. I thought you enjoyed a challenge. What is troubling you?"

John tried to force a smile onto his face. He failed and looked down at his feet. "It's just that everyone else belongs here, sir," he said miserably. "They were *chosen*. I'm just an accident."

"Are you sorry that you were invited to stay on at Hyperspace High?"

"No, no. It's not that," John babbled. "It's just I'm afraid the scholars will tell me to leave. That's what's bothering me. This is the best school *ever*."

"I'm glad you think so," Lorem said. "Accidents often have unexpected consequences. In fact, many people believe the existence of the universe itself is a vast cosmic accident. There is no need to worry about your presence here. I am very happy to have you at Hyperspace High, and I know I am not the only one. You belong at this school as much as anyone else."

"Thank you, sir. But ... well ... I'm not the best student." John lifted up his eyes and looked into the headmaster's face. "Will there be lots of difficult tests?"

An enigmatic smile crossed Lorem's face. "What is life other than a series of tests, John?" the headmaster said. "Tests we must face with courage."

CHAPTER 4

The headmaster's words had an immediate effect. Feeling much more cheerful, John rushed headlong through the docking port after his classmates. Lorem was right, he decided. The inspection was a challenge, and he wasn't going to pass any tests by moaning and being gloomy. *Besides*, he thought to himself, *the first test is Space Flight and Sergeant Jegger says I'm almost as good as Emmie.*

A whistle escaped his lips as he entered the Kerallin spaceship. Inside, the pyramid was a vast single room. Its triangular walls stretched far above John's head and appeared to be made of clear glass, shimmering with a faint purple glimmer.

"Wowsers," he whispered softly to himself. Through

the clear walls and floor of the pyramid, stars blazed in every direction. In the distance, a huge nebula hung in the darkness, a wispy cloud of gases studded with newborn stars. Beneath his feet a comet flashed past, a tail of ice and rock particles flaring behind.

"John, *John*, stop gawping. Come and look at this."

Dropping his gaze from the glories of space, John looked around. Across the ship, Kaal was waving him over. Surrounded by a ring of MorphSeats, he and the rest of the students were huddled around something at the centre of the pyramid.

"Coming!" John walked towards them. Whatever the ship was made of, John knew it must be stronger than any metal found on Earth, but a small part of his brain couldn't help but think that there was only a thin sheet of glass between him and the freezing vacuum. Behind, a grinding sound followed by a loud clank told him that Hyperspace High's docking system had been retracted. He glanced back nervously. The wall was now a flat, unmarked surface with no sign of any docking machinery.

Suddenly, boosters fired, moving the pyramid into space. John stopped, watching for a moment as the elegant white bulk of Hyperspace High disappeared into space in the blink of an eye. The class was now truly on its own, drifting through space in a ship that none of the students had ever flown before with no idea of where they were supposed to go. John couldn't help smiling when he remembered that at his last school the pupils weren't even allowed out of the school gates on their own.

"Hurry *up*, John."

"What are you looking at?" John asked as he got closer.

Kaal pointed.

John's gaze dropped to the floor. Set in a square, four symbols glowed white on the transparent floor. "What are they?" he asked.

"We're not sure," said Kaal. "Hoped you might have some idea."

"Don't look at me."

"They're obviously the ship's controls, you morons," said Mordant Talliver. The half-Gargon boy pushed other students aside with his tentacles. "Here, let me show you."

He jumped on one of the glowing symbols and

looked up expectantly.

Nothing happened. Outside the view of the stars remained unchanged.

Mordant waved his arms and tentacles.

He jumped onto another symbol. And then another.

The ship remained motionless.

"Must be broken," he snapped. "This ship's a heap of junk." Turning away, he threw himself into a MorphSeat, which immediately shaped itself around his body.

Ignoring Mordant's outburst, Emmie stepped forward onto one of the symbols. "There must be a way to getting this thing to move," she said thoughtfully. "You can't have a ship without a way to fly it, and Lorem said this is a test of our problem-solving abilities."

"How about we split up and see if we can find anything that might help?" John suggested.

"That is an *excellent* idea," said Raytanna, a girl with smooth white skin, a tiny mouth, and six large, black eyes. "Emmie is correct – all spacecraft must have some type of propulsion system as well as controls. Our task is to identify how this ship is configured and adapt our knowledge to operate it." With a sideways glance at Mordant, she added, "As its purpose is to test us, its unlikely to be as easy as jumping up and down and waving our tentacles about."

Pretending he hadn't heard, Mordant leaned back in his MorphSeat. He closed his eyes and put his hands behind his head.

Emmie nodded. "Exactly, Raytanna," she said. "Small groups. Let's take a wall each while one group checks over the floor."

"Hey, what's this?" John shouted a while later. He was halfway along the pyramid wall that he, Emmie, and Kaal had chosen to investigate. Etched into the glass were flowing lines, so fine they could barely be seen. Reminding John of ancient Egyptian hieroglyphs, they seemed to be half-words, half-pictures. Apart from the symbols on the floor, they were the only useful things that anyone had found. Within moments, John was surrounded.

Raytanna leaned over, studying the markings with her six eyes. "It appears that these are words. I must confess, however, that I am ignorant as to which language they are written in." She sounded almost ashamed.

"Hey, it's OK, Raytanna. You can't know *everything*," said John, hiding his disappointment. Raytanna was constantly studying. While he and Emmie were always at the bottom of the class, she and Mordant were always at the top. With Mordant refusing to help, it was unlikely that anyone else would be able to translate the words.

At Hyperspace High, the ship's computer translated every word into each student's native tongue, and students wore mobile devices to do the same when they were away from the school. With such advanced technology, John could never see the point of studying Cosmic Languages. But now, he was beginning to understand; these markings were clearly an obsolete language, too ancient to be translated by the computer.

At the back of the small crowd, Emmie cleared her throat. "I've been doing a lot of extra work on Cosmic Languages," she said. "Maybe I could have a look."

"You could give it a go, I suppose," said Lishtig doubtfully, as Emmie knelt and ran her fingers across the faint lines. "But if Raytanna can't read it, I don't fancy your chances much."

Emmie shot him a sharp look.

"Do you recognize it, Emmie?" asked Raytanna. "It looks a little like ancient Kartoxian."

Emmie shook her head. "No, I think it's Lurscript. It looks similar, but is different from Kartoxian. I learned a few words last week. It's still used in parts of the Omega Sector."

"You can *read* it?" Lishtig sounded astonished. This time, the whole class turned to glare. "Sorry, shutting up now."

"I only learned the basics," said Emmie. She pointed at the first word-picture. "This means something like 'make sure'." Her finger moved along the line. "To make ... no ... to *use* or put on." She sat back on her heels, flummoxed. "I think the last word says 'coat'."

"Make sure to put on a coat?" said Lishtig. "Why? Is it cold on Kerallin?"

"*Lishtig!*" Kaal and John said together.

Emmie sighed. "Sorry, that doesn't help much, does it?" she said, getting to her feet. "I should have forced myself to study harder."

"*Force!*" yelped John suddenly. "That's it!"

CHAPTER 5

It was John's turn to become the centre of attention. Every student looked at him curiously.

"Thrust. Lift. Gravity. Drag," John babbled. "The four forces."

"What are you talking about?" asked Kaal, staring at John as if he'd gone mad.

John was already running back towards the symbols on the floor. Over his shoulder, he shouted, "It's just like Jegger always says!"

A few moments later, he was standing breathless on a symbol that looked like a balloon. "This is lift," he said, as the rest of the class made their way over, still confused.

"Still not sure what you're jabbering on about," said Kaal.

John took a deep breath and tried to calm himself. "Sergeant Jegger says that space flight is about balancing four forces – lift, thrust, gravity, and drag." Pointing at his feet, he said, "Lift." John moved his finger to point at the next symbol, a barbell. "That must be drag. Emmie stand there."

Understanding was beginning to dawn in Emmie's eyes. She stepped forward and stood on the symbol next to John. "That means ..." she trailed off, seeing John pointing his finger at the third symbol.

"Fountain ... water ... a *jet* of water. Thrust! Kaal, that's thrust. You stand there. Lishtig, the last one must be gravity. You take that one."

As Lishtig stepped onto the last symbol, a loud chime sounded. Beneath the four students' feet the symbols glowed brightly, rising to float above the floor, and lifting the students with them. Crackles of purple light crawled across the glass pyramid. Waving his arms and wobbling, John only just managed to keep from falling. "Whoa!" he said. "It really *is* all about balance."

"Initiating flight systems," interrupted a light, friendly voice. *The ship's computer*, John guessed.

"Nice one, John," Queelin said.

"Not bad for bottom of the class, " Kaal added.

"I don't want to be a killjoy, but we're still not actually moving," Emmie chipped in.

"Computer: any chance you can tell us how to fly this thing?" asked John.

Silence.

"Worth a try," he shrugged. "OK, then. If it's about balance, then maybe if I make myself shorter than the rest of you by doing *this* ..." He crouched. Instantly, the symbol he was standing on sank towards the floor, while, opposite, Lishig's rose higher. Stars streamed past outside as the pyramid shot upward.

"Brilliant," said Werril admiringly, as John stood up again, bringing the pyramid to a stop. Werril shook his head, with its rhinoceros-like horn growing out of his dark-green face. "So basically, you're balancing out the forces between the four of you to fly the craft."

John nodded. "I think so. We'll need to experiment, though." Looking over his shoulder, he said, "Why don't the rest of you take a seat. This could be a bumpy ride."

Within seconds, the remaining students were strapped into MorphSeats. While they prepared for the flight, Mordant opened his eyes. "Took you long enough to work it out," he drawled, as if all along he had known how to fly the pyramid but couldn't be bothered to tell everyone else. "It's a ridiculously low-tech system," he added. before pretending to doze off again.

The rest of the students were too excited to take any notice.

"Ready?" John asked. Seeing them all nod, he continued. "Kaal, you're thrust. Get us moving."

Kaal bobbed down quickly. *Too* quickly. There were screams as the pyramid shot forward, throwing students back in their seats. On the opposite side, Emmie's symbol threw her into the air. "Watch it, Kaal!" she yelled, only just managing to keep her footing.

"Yee-*hah*!" Kaal shouted in delight. "More speed." He crouched even lower, chuckling as the pyramid flashed through the stars. Emmie wobbled again, a grin spreading across her face.

Steadying himself, John let his knees bend a little. The pyramid's course curved upward. Ready this time, Lishtig spread his arms to balance.

"Emmie!"

Smoothly, Emmie went into a crouch. Students groaned as the pyramid slowed down. As Kaal stood up, Emmie dipped lower and it began to go backward.

"I always said you're a real drag, Emmie ," Lishtig cracked, making the class groan.

"Stop making stupid jokes and help us fly this thing!" Emmie shot back. As she stood, Kaal's symbol dipped again, causing the spaceship to leap forward.

Lishtig crouched and stood, crouched and stood, making the pyramid swerve crazily, to the delight of its passengers.

"This is serious, Lishtig!" shouted Emmie, laughing. "We're being tested, remember?"

"Oh, yeah. Sorry, forgot about that bit." Lishtig stood smoothly, grinning.

Before long the four of them had learned to move together, making the pyramid fly where they wanted it to go. "OK, we seem to have got the hang of it now," John said. The four pilots stood up at the same time. The pyramid cruised to a complete stop.

"So far, so good," agreed Kaal. "But how on Derril do we find Kerallin?"

As the words left his mouth, light blazed a metre above his head. Students gasped as they looked upward. A holographic cube hung in the air; a cube that looked like a 3-D maze made of white neon light. In one corner blinked a purple pyramid.

John ducked instinctively, afraid that the huge puzzle was going to fall on his head. The pyramid shot upward again. As it did so, the small flashing pyramid in the maze moved, too.

"I believe it is a map, showing us the way to Kerallin," said Raytanna. "If we pilot the ship to the centre of the maze, we will arrive at our destination. The small pyramid tracks our progress."

"Sounds sensible," said John, staring up at the shining cube. "But I'm already getting a pain in the neck from staring up at it. Everyone sitting down will have to direct us."

"That will also be part of the test," Raytanna replied. "It seems the scholars have created these trials to make us work as a team. Ingenious."

"Let's go to Kerallin, then," said John with a grin. "Which way first?"

"Straight ahead!" a few of the students yelled back.

Laughing, Kaal went into a crouch while Emmie stood straight. The strange purple spaceship rushed through space.

"Straight ahead for three light years."

"Ninety-degree right turn."

Soon the students were all shouting at once. Unable to stop laughing, John, Emmie, Kaal, and Lishtig did their best to follow the directions. The flight proved so much fun that even Mordant eventually joined in. "You're going the wrong way!" he would shout occasionally, or "Stand up, Tarz, you idiot, you're making the ship as slow as you are." Everyone was having too good a time to care about the occasional snide remark. John caught himself wondering what sort of test could be so much fun.

However, in spite of the jokes, the pyramid was making progress. Every time John craned his neck to look up, the tracker had moved deeper into the 3-D maze.

"Is it much further?" he moaned. "My knees—"

"It may be that the scholars of Kerallin are testing your physical fitness, John," interrupted Raytanna.

"Hey, where's the tracker gone?" Queelin shouted behind him suddenly. "It just blinked and vanished."

"Is this another test?" Lishtig asked.

"What's happening?" John looked over his shoulder to where his classmates were staring up at the cube in confusion.

"Umm ... I think we're here," said Kaal quietly.

A hush descended.

John turned back and followed his friend's pointing finger. Dead ahead was a planet, as green as an emerald and draped with clouds. Three small moons spun around it.

"Autopilot engaged," said the ship's computer. "Prepare for landing on Kerallin."

The pyramid landed in what looked like a wide meadow with barely a bump. Instantly, a section of the wall began to flow and change. Ripples spread across the glass, as a small circular hole appeared. The hole rapidly widened until it was a became a doorway large enough for the students to walk through two abreast.

Still giggling, the class spilled out onto Kerallin. As John passed through the doorway, he looked around in wonder. The planet's green colour obviously came from its lush foliage. In the distance he could see tall trees, heavy with what appeared to be summer leaves. Beneath his feet, jewel-like wild flowers blossomed in a thick carpet of green grass. A stream wound its way through the meadow, and a sun burned bright in the blue sky. John closed his eyes and turned his face to it, feeling the warm rays of a real sun for the first time since the class had visited the museum planet Archivus Major.

Almost like home, he thought.

"That must be where the scholars live," Emmie said, pointing her finger.

On the horizon, slender towers of golden stone glowed in the sunshine. Tall and slim, each was topped with a graceful spire. Beyond them was an enormous domed building.

Stretching his legs, John took a few steps, trying to work the stiffness from his knees. The air was fresh and full of delicate scents. He took a deep lungful.

"Good morning."

The voice was so quiet, John thought for a moment that he had imagined it but, turning his head, he saw two figures walking slowly across the grass. Behind them, a sleek, silver craft with an open top hovered above the ground.

Kaal nudged him. In an awed voice, he whispered, "The scholars of Kerallin!"

CHAPTER 6

As the scholars approached, John looked closely. He was surprised to see that, although both were wearing long academic robes and looked so frail and ancient that a strong wind might blow them over, they were very different to each other. The scholar who had spoken had a large, bulbous head, wrinkled with papery purple skin, and ringed with blinking eyes. He stood slightly taller than the second, a frail, six-armed female who was hunched over, John assumed from the weight of her years. So thin, she looked almost like a walking skeleton, she leaned on the purple-skinned scholar's arm as she shuffled forward.

"Welcome to Kerallin. I am Socrat," wheezed the purple-skinned scholar, as the two stopped before the class. He inclined his head towards the other scholar. "This is Aristil."

"It appears Sergeant Jegger has done a commendable job educating you in Space Flight," said Aristil, looking along the row of students. John leaned forward, straining to hear her soft voice. Aristil's eyes, he noticed, glittered with intelligence. "You made the trip in two hours and sixteen minutes," she went on. "The second-fastest time ever."

Kaal nudged John again. "Well done," he whispered from the corner of his mouth.

"You would all benefit from some extra tuition in Cosmic Languages, however," the six-armed scholar continued, looking less pleased. "None of you managed to translate the instruction to activate the ship's cloaking device."

John heard a sharp intake of breath behind him. "I'm so *dumb*," Emmie hissed. "'Cloaking device', not '*coat*'."

"Further tests will start in the assembly hall in one hour," said Socrat. "In the meantime, we thought you might enjoy a short tour of the planet. Refreshments have been provided on our hoverbus. Please board here."

With wind whipping through his hair, John gazed over Kerallin as the gleaming craft skimmed across the planet. They had passed the complex of towers, learning from Socrat that each housed a different department of study, and flown through carefully tended gardens containing plants from hundreds of worlds. Now the hoverbus sped along a river valley of lush green. An astonishing variety of animals had come to the water's edge to drink, wash, and play. As the hoverbus flashed by, John thought he saw a pink elephant-like creature trumpeting water into the air. He turned to stare, but the animal was already out of sight.

"Mmmm, this is good," he said, lowering his drink.

On the seat in front of him, Aristil turned. "Goldberry juice," she told him. "Goldberries are the only fruit that is native to this planet and only grow in Kerallin's equatorial regions. Unless you return as a scholar one day, you will almost certainly never taste them again."

"I thought the scholars were – you know – a single

species," said Emmie, "and Kerallin was their home world."

"Oh no," Aristil answered in a quivering voice. "Kerallin was an uninhabited dust planet before the first scholars terraformed it." She waved at the animals. "Like most of the plants and all the wildlife, the scholars have arrived here from every corner of the universe." She smiled. "Kerallin is a retreat for the universe's greatest thinkers, a place to continue their studies in peace when they decide to retire from the cares of the universe."

"You mean it's one big, brainy old peoples' home?" John blurted. Realizing how rude that sounded, he blushed. "Sorry, that came out wrong ..."

"Never be afraid to call something what is really is," Aristil replied with another smile. "Yes, Kerallin is 'one big, brainy old peoples' home', though we 'old people' like to tell ourselves that we still do useful work."

"What did *you* do, before you came here?" Emmie asked.

"Me, my dear? Why, I was headmistress of Hyperspace High." Seeing the looks of astonishment on the students' faces, Aristil laughed. "I haven't always been as old as this," she said, her eyes glittering. For a split second John could see that she had once been very beautiful. "Ah," the scholar continued, "our tour is up. Here's the assembly hall. Let's see what you have learned at Hyperspace High, shall we?"

The hoverbus stopped at the bottom of a set of wide steps leading up to the grandest of the towers. The students made their way up to an ornately carved doorway, where exotic flowers bloomed on each side. Now that they were actually on Kerallin and about to face the scholars in person, most were nervous. Only Mordant climbed the steps as if he didn't have a care in the world.

"I didn't study hard enough, I didn't study hard enough," Raytanna repeated to herself over and over. Her normally smooth forehead was creased with worry.

"Raytanna, the only time you don't study is when you eat," Werril told her.

Emmie gripped John's arm. He looked into her terrified eyes. "What is life but a series of tests?" he said gently. "We can only face them with courage."

"John," Emmie whispered.

"Yes?"

"Please shut up."

John grinned. "It sounded better when the headmaster said it," he said. "Come on, you'll be fine. Kaal and I will be right next to you."

Together, the three of them stepped through the doorway. Globes of light illuminated a passageway, which was lined with holographic portraits of past scholars. Whispering quietly, the students walked through, footsteps echoing on the marble floor. A soft gasp ran through the class as it reached the main chamber of the assembly hall.

The walls were covered in rich carvings, representing all the different academic fields. John understood only a tiny fraction, but here and there were mathematical laws that he had seen before. Soft light filtered through tall windows of coloured glass that were arranged in strange, but beautiful, patterns. At one end of the room was a raised platform. Higher still, a semicircle of twenty throne-like carved chairs looked down upon it. Every chair was occupied.

"The students will approach the dais and wait to

be called upon," boomed a voice from the far end of the hall.

"This isn't at all nerve-racking," joked Lishtig, as the class stepped across deep rugs and lined up before the platform.

John had been feeling nervous before Lorem's calming words. Looking up at the scholars in their massive thrones, his nerves now threatened to become outright terror. The scholars of Kerallin, it seemed, had gone out of their way to make the students feel as small as possible. Aristil had taken a seat at one end, and Socrat at the other. Between them were eighteen scholars from eighteen different planets. Only their academic robes were the same. Most were creatures that John had never seen before. One had a face that looked like an intricate silver mask; another's body was covered in long spikes. About halfway along was an elderly Derrilian, his red eyes full of curiosity and fixed on Kaal.

"Each of you will step onto the dais and answer a single question in turn," the voice said. John wondered where it was coming from. None of the scholars had spoken. "First, Mordant Talliver."

John watched as the black-haired half-Gargon mounted the steps. Mordant stood at ease, as if he owned the planet, gazing up at the scholars with confidence.

A tiny being with fish-scale skin and the most enormous pair of spectacles John had ever seen spoke first. "I am Scholar Ulara Forshart. Mordant Talliver, translate for me the phrase, '*Eshli car shou torashla y eshli cerashadil cormawan.*'"

Mordant answered in a heartbeat. "Those who have knowledge speak, but those who have wisdom listen," he said. "It is ancient Elvian, Scholar Forshart. One of the sayings of the philosopher Volaxian Hardesh."

"Very good. You may step down, Mordant."

"I *knew* that," whispered Emmie at John's side. "Why couldn't they give *me* that one."

John squeezed her hand.

When Mordant had stepped back into line, the old Derrilian spoke. "Lishtig ar Steero."

"Oh boy, here we go," muttered Lishtig, as he climbed the steps.

"Good morning, Lishtig, I am Scholar Deem," said the Derrilian. "In biology, DNA carries the genetic code for over eighty per cent of all galactic life forms. But for which three advanced species do silipeteronuclaic cells, also known as SPCs, perform the same function?"

Lishtig glanced back at Gobi-san-Art. "Well, the Koo-rag-tar is one. I know that because one of them's my best mate," he said.

The corner of the Derrilian's mouth twitched.

"Umm … the other two are … hang on, I know this … the Skar of planet Tharlon Four … and … and the Ghuremalite of planet Ghurem."

"Indeed. Thank you, Lishtig."

"Raytanna Vitor," said the mask-faced scholar.

Raytanna took her place on the platform, head hanging and her hands gripped into fists at her side.

"I am Scholar Silva, Raytanna. In robotics, how many degrees of freedom are required in the construction of a fully working humanoid hand?"

Raytanna's head jerked up. "But that's *easy!*" she exclaimed. "Every textbook agrees that twenty degrees of freedom are necessary, but I have been running my own tests, which suggest an extra two degrees in the carpal region would give additional strength and flexibility. In addition—"

"Thank you, Raytanna. You may step down now," the scholar interrupted.

"Sorry, sorry," Raytanna gabbled.

"Not at all. Your research sounds fascinating. We must find time to speak before you leave."

Kaal was next. Despite his earlier confidence, he was visibly shaking as he stood before the scholars. John knew that his shy room-mate hated being the centre of attention.

From the corner of his eye, John saw the elderly Derrilian flash three fingers at Kaal – a Derrilian thumbs-up – and then cover the movement by scratching his nose. For the first time since entering the hall, John felt himself smile.

Kaal's question was on astrophysics. John knew it wasn't one of his friend's best subjects, but the hunched Elvian scholar seemed satisfied with his answer and told Kaal to return to his place.

"Cool, well done, mate," John whispered as Kaal stood next to him, wiping sweaty palms on his uniform.

"John Riley."

On legs of jelly, John stepped up onto the dais.

I won't let them see how nervous I am.

Straightening his posture, John lifted his chin and clasped his hands behind his back.

"An Earthling," wheezed a particularly old being – a tiny creature with grey, spotted skin and a nose that hung down to his waist. "We've never had an Earthling before, have we?"

John felt a blush rise to his face as a number of the scholars leaned forward to inspect him.

"They call themselves human beings, Thushlar. He's the first to attend Hyperspace High," said Socrat.

"Earthlings, human beings – can't they make their minds up?" wheezed the old being. "Never mind, never mind. As you have probably gathered, I am Scholar Thushlar. Tell me, what is the square root of three million, nine-hundred and twenty-eight thousand, three hundred and twenty-four?"

John's shoulders slumped with relief. Maths was by far his best subject. Numbers were the same in every galaxy, and he had always had a talent for solving mathematical problems. Even so, it was a fiendishly difficult question to tackle without a calculator.

Break it down … Factorize into prime numbers …

pair ... carry over ... check the result ... check again ...

"One thousand, nine hundred, and eighty-two, sir."

Thushlar sat back in his throne. "Correct," he said. "Fast. I like that in a mathematician."

"Thank you, Scholar Thushlar."

"And polite, too. Maybe Hyperspace High should get more of these Earthling human beings."

Liking the wheezy old alien more and more, John grinned up at him.

"That will do, *for now*, John Riley. Back to your place."

Emmie was the last to face the scholars. By the time she climbed the steps, John could tell she was a nervous wreck. Unable to hold herself still, she folded her arms, then put them behind her back, then pushed silver hair out of her eyes.

It seemed that the scholars had also noticed. "Emmie Tarz," Aristil said gently, "in the third Quesney War, what was the name of the general who led the rebel Parshian forces?"

John winced. Of all the subjects the scholars could have chosen for Emmie, Hyperspace History was the worst. She hated it and constantly confused the names and dates of important events. Aristil might as well have asked her to name every soldier who took part in the third Quesney War. He glanced up at Kaal, who shook his head. There was nothing they could do.

On stage, Emmie stood in absolute silence. John could only see the back of her head, but he knew she would be biting her lip. He felt a horrible tight feeling in his chest as he watched his friend tremble.

Silence.

"I'm afraid I will have to hurry you."

"I-I d-don't ... ugh ... is it ... no, n-not h-him."

"Emmie Tarz?"

"*General Looshid*!" Emmie blurted.

Aristil frowned. "That answer is incorrect."

"It was General Kaskov!" shouted Mordant. "General Trutley bo Kaskov."

The scholars ignored him. As one they stood. At the end of the line, Socrat took a step forward. "For the next test, we invite you all to visit our library. If you would kindly follow Aristil and myself."

Tears ran down Emmie's face as she slipped back into her place. John put an arm around her shoulders.

"It's OK, Emmie," said Kaal. "They're not going to

fail you for one wrong answer."

"You don't *know* that, Kaal," she answered, her eyes sparkling with tears of pale blue. "What if they do? And there's more tests yet to come. I'm bound to get all those wrong, too. What if they ask me to leave? Even worse, what if they fail the entire class? If Hyperspace High fails an inspection for the first time ever, it will be all my fault."

CHAPTER 7

John hardly noticed where Aristil and Socrat were leading. Emmie had dried her eyes, but her shoulders remained slumped. She walked in gloomy silence as the two scholars shuffled slowly through gardens overflowing with strange and beautiful blooms, her eyes fixed on the path ahead. On either side of her, John and Kaal exchanged worried glances.

"The Library of Kerallin," said Socrat. "Here, all the knowledge of the universe is stored."

John jumped. Wrapped up in his own thoughts, he hadn't noticed that the class had arrived at the domed building he had noticed earlier. Up close, it was enormous – a small village could easily have been built inside – and the only modern-looking building among the towers.

A flicker of green light washed over the old scholar's face, as a hidden retina scanner checked his identity.

"Socrat of Tersia Prime," said an electronic voice. "Enter."

The doors swung open.

John had been expecting a library similar to Hyperspace High's, where ancient books were kept behind glass and students could view their contents on ThinScreens. Instead, the sight that met his eyes was unlike anything he'd ever imagined. At his side, even Emmie breathed, "Wow" under her breath and gazed around in wonder.

Gleaming shelves reached to the ceiling. Not one held a book. Every shelf was separated into small compartments, and every compartment was occupied by a shining ball of coloured light. There were hundreds of globes on the shelves he could see, and, at the centre of the library, even more rows radiated outward like spokes on a wheel.

"What are they?" he whispered.

On either side, Emmie and Kaal looked baffled. "No idea," said Kaal, staring at the glimmering balls above his head. "I've never seen anything like it."

Aristil walked forward and took a globe from the nearest shelf in one of her many hands. Turning back to face the class, she ran another hand across its glowing red surface. Instantly, the globe grew until it was the size of a beachball.

"It looks like a planet," said Emmie.

"This time, you are quite correct, Emmie," the scholar said. "The planet Yaroh Tar, to be exact. The globe contains the essence of the world – its rocks and mountains, its underground lakes, and, of course, its complete history."

Stepping forward to stand at her side, Socrat waved a hand towards the stacked shelves. "The library contains a globe for every planet in the universe," he said, with a hint of pride in his voice. "You will find nothing like it anywhere else in the universe."

"I d-don't understand," Kaal stuttered. "Those aren't holograms. The technology to make something like that doesn't exist, *anywhere*."

Socrat leaned forward, his already quiet voice

dropping to a whisper. "Young Derrilian," he said, "the scholars of Kerallin choose when to share their discoveries and inventions with the universe. So far, we have not chosen to share our library. In the wrong hands, the power of such knowledge would be very dangerous indeed."

Aristil clapped her hands together, the noise echoing from the shelves. "Your next task," she said, "is to prepare a Galactic Geography presentation. You will use the globe that represents your home world to prepare a presentation for the scholars. Extra marks will be given to those who are able to tell us something that extends our own knowledge. The best presentation will win a special award."

John's hand shot up. "Can you ... errr ... tell us where to find the right globes? There must be thousands in here," he said.

Aristil smiled again. She and Socrat began shuffling towards the exit. "It wouldn't be much of a test if we gave you all the answers now, would it?" she said.

"Don't take too long finding your planets!" Socrat called over his shoulder. "The presentations begin in three hours."

The students spread out, gazing up in awe at the tiny glowing planets. "A special award," said Emmie in an excited whisper. "Did you hear that? Aristil said there would be a special award for the best presentation. If I win, I might still pass the inspection."

"Good thinking," John replied. "But first we need to find the right globes. It could take days."

Up ahead, Lishtig leaned over a shelf. "Hey, this one says it's planet Fy-Ix-Cero," he shouted. "Anyone here from Fy-Ix-Cero?"

Seeing the students around him shake their heads, he grinned. "Oh well, only another few thousand to get through." He moved along to the next globe. "How about Garshom Ssvene?"

"The planets must be organized in a logical system," Raytanna said, running a long, white finger along a shelf. "We only need to understand that system."

"Maybe they're arranged alphabetically?" John suggested.

Kaal shook his head. "It would be impossible to arrange so many worlds alphabetically," he said. "For a start, most of them have different languages, some of which are impossible to translate."

"Perhaps they're organized by size," said Emmie, wandering up to the centre of the library, where a ring of glowing circular panels were set in the floor, surrounded by desks and MorphSeats. "What's the biggest planet in the universe?"

"No," said Raytanna thoughtfully. "Too many planets would be similar in size. It must be something else."

By now, Kaal had reached the end of the row. "Hey!" he shouted back. "Every row has a number! Look! This one is zero-zero-one, the next row is zero-zero-two, and so on."

The other students clustered around him. "How's that supposed to help us?" asked Werril doubtfully.

Kaal's straightened up, his eyes shining. "I've got it!" he shouted. "It's obvious when you think about it. The planets are arranged by planetary number. Each row is a different galaxy, and the globes must be numbered according to their solar system and position." Turning to Emmie, he said, "What's Silar's planetary number?"

Emmie looked at him blankly. "Is that something I'm supposed to know?" she asked.

Kaal sighed. "Silar is in the Zeta Galaxy, that's the twenty-fourth." He ran to row zero-two-four. "There are six hundred and thirty-seven solar systems in that region. Silar orbits Skylara, number three-eight-two." Kaal's forehead creased in concentration as he counted shelves. "Oh, they're grouped into hundreds, that's sensible," he muttered. Raising his voice, he shouted, "How many planets in the Skylara system, Emmie?"

"Oh, I know that," Emmie replied brightly. "Six, Silar is the second."

"So the planetary number is zero-two-four-point-three-eight-two-point-zero-two," he said, reaching up to a shelf. "And here's Silar."

"Brilliant, Kaal," said Emmie, as he dropped the small globe into her hands. "Now all we've got to do is find out how these things work."

The library filled with excited whoops as students scurried down rows and found their own planets. Only John was left looking around, still baffled. "Umm ... I have no idea what Earth's planetary number is, either," he said nervously.

Kaal grinned. "Luckily for you, Mars is one of the

most famous planets in the universe. I know its number by heart. We'll just find that and Earth will be the next one along the shelf."

Earth's globe was on a top shelf, near the top of the domed ceiling.

"Are we supposed to climb up the shelves?" John asked, frowning.

"You could try that, I suppose," answered Kaal. "Or you could ask a friend who just happens to have a magnificent set of wings." The Derrilian's huge wings snapped out.

"Umm … Kaal. Do you think flying's such a good idea in here?" Emmie said.

She was too late. Kaal had already leapt upward, his leathery wings thrashing. Swirling gusts of air blew John and Emmie's hair back, as their friend flew towards the ceiling.

"*Kaal!*" Emmie shrieked, as the first globe fell.

"Look out!" cried Emmie. " You're creating too much turbulence."

John dived, catching the precious globe just before it hit the floor. Another plummeted downward. "*Kaal!*" Emmie screamed again, as she plucked the globe out of the air. "Come down ... Oh no, John. There's another—"

"Got it." John caught another globe, as Emmie put hers gently on the floor and ran backward, her eyes fixed on another globe that had been blown off its shelf by Kaal's flapping wings. "Quick Emmie, two more coming!" John shouted.

"What were you two shouting about?" asked Kaal a few moments later as he landed lightly, another globe in his hands. "I couldn't hear you up there ... Oww, *Emmie*. What was that for?" he finished, as Emmie pushed him roughly to one side.

Emmie caught a globe that would have smashed on Kaal's head and held it before his eyes. "Oops," said Kaal, noticing the other fallen spheres and looking sheepish. "Did I ...? Are any ..."

"We got them all," Emmie replied with a raised eyebrow. "But don't do that again."

"We are such idiots. Look, there's a lift here," said John, dragging over a platform on wheels and replacing the fallen globes.

"Oops ... Well, anyway, here's Earth," said Kaal, passing John the globe he had fetched.

John immediately forgot about the near-catastrophe. Before his eyes was a tiny Earth. Clouds moved slowly over the familiar shape of continents: the Americas, Africa, Europe, Asia, Australia. John reached out and gently touched the shape of Britain. *Home.*

"Thankfully, there's no damage done," said Emmie, interrupting John's thoughts. "Come on, let's get on with the presentations."

Each carrying their own planet, the three of them hurried back to the centre of the library. There, Raytanna had discovered that placing a globe above one of the glowing floor panels allowed the planet to float in the air. Most of the students were already running their hands over the surfaces of their globes, calling out advice to their neighbours.

"Spinning makes time go backward and forward!" called Werril.

"And you can zoom in and out by tapping on an area," added Gobi. "Like in the holo-lab back at school."

The Earth globe was light in John's hands and grew slightly in size when he stroked the surface. He slid a hand across its surface again and stepped back quickly as it increased to the size of a weather balloon.

"Cool, Queelin, your planet looks like one big desert. Look at the size of those sand dunes." John looked up to see Lishtig with his nose pressed close to Queelin's globe.

"It *is* a desert," Queelin replied. She pointed. "We have some water, though. Look, here's Oasis City, where I live. It's built around the biggest pool on the planet."

Despite the three-hour deadline for their presentations, most of the students were curious to see their classmates' home planets and were eagerly walking around looking at the different worlds. Only Mordant was busy working with his own globe. Half-Gargon, half-Tiqlar, he had chosen Gargon for his presentation. From across the circle, the planet looked dark and gloomy to John.

Unable to resist, John peered at Kaal's world. Derril was a planet of grey craggy mountains and steep cliffs. Trees rose as high as skyscrapers from deep gorges filled with dense vegetation. Here and there, John could see Derrilians swooping through the sky, landing on balconies of elegantly built wooden "nests" that were built into cliff faces.

Turning, John looked over Emmie's shoulder. "That's beautiful!" he gasped. Candy-floss clouds, tinged with pink, drifted across continents of pale yellows and greens. Here and there were ranges of snow-capped mountains, waterfalls tumbling into wide lakes and rivers.

"Thanks," said Emmie shyly. "Some people call Silar the 'Jewel of the Galaxy'." Peering across at Earth, she continued, "But your planet is spectacular, too. Look at all that water! You're so lucky to have such vast oceans."

John pointed to Britain. "That's the country I live in," he said. "It's completely surrounded by sea." He spun the Earth absent-mindedly, then stared. As Gobi had said, time moved backward. Millions of years passed in the blink of an eye. Continents moved. Now Europe and North America joined together as one huge continent. South America floated free on its own. India moved away from Asia, and the Himalayan Mountains fell to become a flat coast.

Fascinated, John flicked his fingers over North America. Now he could see dense forests and wide plains. Volcanoes spilled fiery rock. John's eyes widened as he zoomed in closer still. A tyrannosaurus rex ran across grassland, roaring in victory as its powerful claws ripped into a hadrosaur. John moved the globe slightly and watched as a pterodactyl launched itself from a cliff.

"Hey, look at that," said Kaal behind him. A thick green finger jabbed towards the pterodactyl over John's shoulder. "That guy looks a bit like me."

"It's a dinosaur, Kaal. They died out millions of years ago," John replied. He spun the globe in the opposite direction and zoomed in on an area of France. A group of dirty-looking men wrapped in animal skins squatted around the body of a mammoth, stripping it with stone knives. "Those are my ancestors: primitive humans," he said in awe.

"I didn't think it was possible for humans to be any more primitive than they are now."

Whirling round, John saw that Mordant had left his own globe and was now staring at Earth, lip curled in a sneer. John's hands balled into fists. While his friends might joke about "primitive" Earthlings, from Talliver's mouth the word sounded exactly as it was meant – like a deadly insult.

"At least Earth looks like a nice place to live," Emmie snapped back before John could speak. "Gargon's one big swamp."

"I'd rather live in a swamp than some pathetic little planet that doesn't even know there are far more intelligent life forms in the universe," Mordant replied. "Wait until you see my presentation on Gargon. With everything my planet's achieved, I can't fail to win the special award."

As the half-Gargon stalked back to his own globe, John forced himself to relax. Spinning Earth once more, he flicked his fingers over Britain. Flicking his fingers again and again, he zoomed in on his town, street, and house.

"This is incredible," he whispered. "The globe is collecting every scrap of information from Earth in real time." Leaning forward, he watched as his dad threw a ball for the new family dog, Super Rover. The little Jack Russell ran across the garden to fetch it.

Kaal and Emmie crowded in to see what he was looking at. "That's my dad," said John in a hoarse voice.

"Wow, your dad's really hairy," said Kaal.

"That's a *dog*, Kaal," John said, laughing. "It's a pet. You know, like Super Rover that I built for the Robot Warriors. That's my dad, there." He pointed.

"Where's your mum?" said Emmie, leaning in so close John could feel her soft hair against his cheek.

John gazed at the scene in front of him. "There," he said quietly, pointing to his mother. She was kneeling in the grass, cutting back the plants before winter set in. As John watched, she lifted her face to the sun and stretched, turning to laugh at something John's dad had just said.

Emmie's fingers curled around John's arm. "Your mum is pretty," she said softly. "She looks so happy. And your dad seems to like making her laugh."

"Yeah, they're both pretty cool," John replied. Tears pricked at his eyes. Seeing his parents always reminded him of how much he missed them.

Stop it, Riley, he warned himself silently. *You are not going to start blubbing in front of everyone.* Standing up straight, he smiled and said to Emmie, "Hey, I'd love to take a look at your—" His sentence went unfinished. An alarm roared, shredding the quiet peace of Kerallin's library.

CHAPTER 8

Shouts filled the library as the alarm wailed on. The students struggled to make themselves heard over the noise. "What's going on?" John yelled at Kaal.

Kaal shook his head, passing a hand across his face – a gesture John recognized as a Derrilian shrug.

"Is there a fire?" Bareon yelled, looking around anxiously.

Students ran to check the long rows of shelves, but the library looked just as it had a few moments before. Apart from the alarm, there was no sign of an emergency. Slightly confused, they met back at the centre of the library.

"We'd better get out of here, just in case!" John shouted above the noise. "Maybe it's a drill. We should group up outside and wait for the alarm to stop."

Presentations forgotten, the class walked calmly to the doors and lined up on the library steps. Outside, there was still no clue as to what might have triggered the alarm. Strange-looking birds flapped away from the noise through calm blue skies. A light breeze carried the scent of exotic flowers. Apart from the wailing alarm, all was calm and peaceful.

On the library steps, the noise was slightly less deafening. John glanced around at his classmates' worried faces. "What should we do?" he asked Kaal.

"I guess we just stay here, but everything looks fine," Kaal replied. "Maybe someone touched something they shouldn't have. I'm sure someone will come and tell us what's going on in a moment."

"Here they come now," said Emmie. "Look."

On the lawns in front of the library, Aristil and Socrat climbed down from the hoverbus and hurried up the path. Both scholars looked grim and nervous.

"Something's seriously wrong," John said under

his breath. "Is there a problem?" he asked as they came closer.

The scholars glanced at each other and shook their heads, unwilling to share any more. "You must leave immediately," Aristil said, waving all six arms in the air. "Please follow us to the hoverbus. We will take you back to the ship that brought you here. Return to Hyperspace High as fast as you can. The ship will show you the way."

"Why do we have to go?" John blurted out. "What's going on?"

"It is for your own safety," Socrat wheezed.

"But what about our presentations?" asked Emmie.

"There is no time to explain," said Aristil, sharply. "Leave your work. Please, follow us to the hoverbus."

The scholars turned, shuffling towards the hoverbus as fast as they could. Shrugging and exchanging questioning glances, the students followed in silence. John tried asking Aristil what had happened once again as he climbed aboard. His answer was a look that told him firmly that she would not be giving out any information.

The hoverbus shot away at high speed, throwing

those still standing into the laps of their classmates. Still, Aristil and Socrat ignored the students' questions. Leaning their heads together at the front of the hoverbus , the scholars whispered to each other. John couldn't hear what they were saying above the wind, but the tone of their voices was unmistakably urgent.

As John gazed across the landscape of Kerallin, the scene outside looked as tranquil as it had when they had landed.

"Maybe there's a big storm coming," suggested Bareon. "Or an earthquake or something."

"Don't be daft, Bareon." Sprawled across the back seat, Lishtig was the only student who looked relaxed. His long ponytail streamed behind him in the breeze. "I bet you a slice of Falarcake at Ska's Café we were so totally awesome the scholars decided not to bother with any more tests," he said brightly.

"More likely Tarz has already earned us a fail," said Mordant.

Lishtig raised an eyebrow. "Is there any situation you can't make worse just by opening your mouth, Talliver?" he demanded.

Before Mordant could retort, the hoverbus slowed

to a halt at the pyramid ship. As it stopped, the wind dropped. The two scholars didn't appear to notice that their words could now be heard by the students in the seats behind.

"But how did they find Kerallin?" Aristil whispered.

Socrat nodded his purple head towards the pyramid ship. "The students failed to activate the cloaking device," he answered. "It seems they were tracked all the way here from Hyperspace High."

In the seat beside John, Emmie let out a low groan. Her golden skin turned the colour of pale custard.

"I didn't translate the cloaking device instruction," she hissed. "Whatever's happening, it's my fault."

"None of us translated it, Emmie," Kaal replied quickly. "If it caused a problem, we're *all* responsible."

"No talking, please," said Aristil sharply. "Quickly now, board the ship and get away from Kerallin. Please make sure that you activate the cloaking device immediately."

John walked across the grass to the pyramid feeling deeply uneasy. Kaal was right; if something dangerous was happening because the class hadn't turned on the ship's cloak, then all the students were to blame. Running to safety while the elderly scholars dealt with whatever mess the students had caused made him feel like a coward.

"Are you sure we can't stay and help?" he asked Aristil, as most of his classmates took their MorphSeats in the centre of the pyramid. Emmie, Kaal, and Raytanna ran to the far wall, where John had found the cloaking device instruction earlier.

Aristil shook her head. "It was you who first understood how to pilot the pyramid, was it not, John Riley?" she said.

"Uh, yes. Yes, I guess so."

"Then you can help by flying the ship and getting your fellow students away from here as fast as possible."

"But—"

"*Go!*" she ordered.

With no choice but to obey, John followed the rest of the class inside the pyramid.

"Cloak activated," said the ship's computer.

From the inside, nothing looked different – through the shimmering purple-tinged walls, he could still see the landscape of Kerallin. From the little he knew of light-bending cloaking technology, he guessed that the ship had become invisible to anyone looking at it from the outside.

Taking his place opposite Lishtig, John waited while Raytanna fastened her safety harness.

"OK," he said quietly as Emmie and Kaal took their positions. "Let's get out of here."

He was about to duck down and launch the pyramid upward, when Mordant screamed and pointed outside.

John whirled round. A spaceship was falling from the sky like a meteor. Red, and covered with cruel-looking spikes, its landing jets blasted the ground. In the distance, trees bent. Outside the pyramid, Aristil and Socrat huddled inside the hoverbus, their robes whipping wildly in the rush of hot winds. Another hoverbus came speeding across the meadow. Scholars spilled out onto the ground, pointing in panic as the red ship landed, crushing plants and flowers beneath.

A hatch opened. A ramp emerged. Marching two abreast, thirty soldier droids stamped down the ramp and spread out on the grass. Red metal armour, studded with spikes, glinted in the sunshine. Featureless metal faces turned towards the scholars, levelling powerful-looking laser rifles at their shocked faces.

Thushlar collapsed, clutching his chest. Deem, the old Derrilian scholar, caught him before he hit the ground.

John backed across the floor towards his classmates, unable to take his eyes off the scene outside the pyramid. The attack had happened so quickly, it felt like his brain was still trying to catch up.

"What are you waiting for, John, you *idiot*. Get us out of here!" shrieked Mordant.

The words acted like a kick-start. "No!" John yelled as he turned back, pointing wildly at the scholars of Kerallin. "We can't just *leave* them."

Mordant stood, his face red with rage, tentacles thrashing at the air. "Not this time!" he shrieked. "You're not going to try and be the hero this time. The scholars *ordered* us to get away. We have to go. *NOW!*"

"They need help!" John shouted back. "We have to stay."

"Mordant is right," yelled Werril. "We can't fight armed soldier droids, and the scholars told us to go."

97

"I'm not going anywhere," said Lishtig. The purple-haired boy crossed the floor to stand at John's side. "On my world, we don't leave friends in trouble."

"And on *my* world, we don't get caught up in trouble that's none of our business!" shouted Mordant, enraged. "Especially when no one wants us to get involved."

Suddenly, everyone was shouting at once.

"Maybe we should get help!" yelled Bareon.

"It will take too long. The scholars need our help now!" replied Queelin urgently.

"We *can't* fight soldier droids," insisted Mordant.

"I can," said Gobi-san-Art, crossing huge arms that looked like they'd been carved from granite.

"*STOP IT*! STOP SHOUTING!" Kaal bellowed.

Silence descended, as every student turned to the Derrilian. "Whatever we do, we need to make a decision fast," he said. "Fighting among ourselves isn't going to help them." He pointed. Outside, the droids were advancing on the scholars, herding them into a group.

"We'll vote," Emmie cut in. "Everyone for staying." Her own hand was in the air instantly. John, Kaal,

Lishtig, Gobi, Raytanna, and Queelin voted to stay. After a few moments, Bareon put his hand in the air.

"Everyone for leaving," said Emmie. Mordant Talliver and seven others raised hands, tentacles, and claws.

"Eight versus eight," said Emmie. "Who hasn't voted?"

Kritta Askin-Tarsos clicked her insect-like mouthparts nervously, turning her huge compound eyes from Emmie to Mordant.

"It's all down to you then, Kritta," said Emmie. "You *have* to make a decision."

"What would the headmaster want you to do?" John added.

Silence.

Then, in a timid voice, Kritta said, "We stay."

CHAPTER 9

"Keep down. Stay out of sight," John whispered over his shoulder. Ahead, the pyramid's wall rippled. The circular door opened silently. Pressing himself against the wall to one side and holding his breath, John peered round. Now, he could hear as well as see what was happening outside.

The soldier droids were twenty-five metres away, facing the scholars. Red armour gleamed in the bright sunlight.

"Line up. No sudden movements. Any attempts to escape will be met with extreme force," droned one in a flat, electronic voice.

Many of the elderly scholars looked frightened and bewildered as they formed a line. Nevertheless, John noted a few who seemed more angry than scared. From their faces, John guessed that Deem and metal-faced Silva would have preferred to fight.

Good. Maybe we'll have some help.

"This is madness. You're going to get us all killed."

"Shut up, Mordant," hissed Emmie. "The cloaking device is on so they don't know we're here. Let's keep it that way for now."

Keeping low, John turned back to his classmates. "Anyone know where these droids came from or what they want?" he asked.

"There are always a few rogue warlords and space pirates at the edge of every galaxy," Bareon whispered, his huge black eyes blinking. "Maybe one of them sent the droids."

"But why? Why attack a retirement planet for old geniuses?"

"Kerallin is more than that—" Raytanna began.

"Does it matter where they come from or what they want?" hissed Emmie. "Let's just stop them."

John nodded. Emmie was right. He peered around

the door again. On clanking metal legs, the droids were now walking up and down the line of scholars. The droids looked fearsome. A thought popped into John's head: if anyone knew how to beat these robots, it would be Kaal. His room-mate was a genius with technology. "Kaal," he whispered, "any idea how we can beat these things?"

"I don't know this model," the Derrilian answered quietly. "But they have two legs, so we should be able to knock them off balance. Get them on the ground and they'll be easier to fight." He paused for a second, deep in thought as he gazed at the droids. "Their armour is designed to withstand weapon fire, not close combat. There will be weak points at the joints. The simple way to take them down is to grab any wires you see and rip them out. But do it quick."

"What about the laser rifles?"

"Long range," Kaal said with a shrug. "Awkward in hand-to-hand combat but still deadly. Don't let them get off a shot."

"Right," said John. "We'll go in three, two—"

"I AM OGUN. THIS PLANET NOW BELONGS TO ME."

Every head snapped round. Through the transparent walls, John saw a being at the top of the spaceship's ramp. The creature that called itself Ogun was two metres tall and covered in the same red, spiked armour as the droids. But instead of a smooth metal face, Ogun had a head that made him look like a hideous cross between a boar and a dragon. Tusks curled from either side of his mouth. Blood-red, overlapping scales covered his face. Smoke curled from a blunt, aggressive snout. On either side of his forehead were twisted horns, tipped with wicked-looking blades. Between them a golden crest ran down the centre of his scaled head. In one taloned hand, he held a hooked sword of black metal. The other was held in a victorious fist above his head.

"OBEY AND I WILL ALLOW YOU TO LIVE," Ogun roared. "DEFY ME AND YOU WILL SUFFER IN WAYS YOU CANNOT IMAGINE."

"John, even you must see we can't stay and fight now," Mordant hissed in a terrified whisper. "Let's … let's get out of here while we still can."

Weak-kneed, John lifted a hand to silence Mordant. He couldn't take his eyes off Ogun.

"Kerallin," he said in a voice only slightly less than a roar, "soon, I will be the greatest warlord the universe has ever known." Metal boots slammed against the craft's ramp, as Ogun descended, glittering green eyes fixed on the huddle of scholars as he crossed the grass. "The famous scholars ..." he began and then stopped, gazing at Aristil, "... and *you*!" he finished. Throwing his head back, Ogun bellowed laughter at the sky.

Aristil stood calm while Ogun's insane laughter went on and on. Finally, it ended abruptly. Gazing at the old scholar, Ogun said, "It is only fitting that Kerallin's treasures should be delivered into my hands by you, *headmistress*."

Her own eyes cold, Aristil looked back at him unflinching. "I thought I recognized you," she said quietly. "It has been, what, three hundred years?"

"Three hundred and twelve, since you threw me out of Hyperspace High," Ogun replied. He gave her a vicious grin. "As you can see, though, my rise to greatness was not stopped by a stupid old being with no vision to see glory in the making."

"*Glory in the making*?" snapped Aristil. "Is that

what you call it? I remember a boy whose barbaric tastes for causing pain ruined everything he could have achieved."

"Yet see what I have achieved." Ogun used his sword to point back towards the ship. John glanced back, seeing six deep grooves gouged into the spaceship's hull. "You see the scars?" Ogun continued. "One for each planet I have conquered. My empire grows, and, with the knowledge that Kerallin provides me, it will grow more quickly still."

He looked around. "And all because I remembered your humiliating inspections of Hyperspace High. For years I have been watching, waiting for a class that fails to activate the cloaking device. Tracking the pyramid back to Kerallin was easy. Conquering a planet of stuffy old fools will be easier still."

"I knew it. It *is* my fault," groaned Emmie behind John.

"*Our* fault, Emmie," said Kaal. "I told you: none of us managed to translate the cloaking device instruction."

John looked over his shoulder. A number of students were exchanging guilty looks. "That settles it once and for all," he said. "We brought Ogun here. It's up to us to get rid of him."

"John, you fool, look at Ogun," said Mordant, his long tentacles weaving in fear. "He's a heavily armed galactic warlord. We're *students*. We've got no weapons and—"

"Be quiet," hissed Lishtig, "Look, something's happening."

The class turned back to the scholars outside. Socrat had stepped forward. His voice was faint. Students crowded around the door to hear him speak.

"There is nothing for you here, Ogun," the old alien wheezed. "Kerallin is a quiet planet, far from the centre of the universe. We only hope to share our knowledge. What good are a few old academics to you?"

"Do you think me stupid?" sneered the warlord, thick smoke pouring from his nostrils.

"I meant only to say—"

"I know what you meant to say," Ogun roared. "Trickery and lies. You know as well as I that there is treasure on Kerallin far beyond jewels."

"I assure you we have nothing—"

Once again, Ogun cut him off. "You have your library," he bellowed contemptuously. "A library where all the information of the universe is stored. With such a library in my hands, I will know every planet's defence systems: everything I need to conquer whichever planet I chose. None will be able to withstand me. Anyone else who wishes to use my library will have to pay. I shall be powerful and rich beyond dreams." He looked Socrat up and down. "And your age means little. You may be old, but Kerallin is home to the brightest minds in the universe. There will be no more 'peaceful study'. From now on, the scholars of Kerallin will design weapons for me. Weapons more powerful than any in the universe."

Fear and confusion turned to shock on the faces of the scholars. "Never!" shouted Socrat, his voice stronger now. "I will never lift a finger to help you."

"THEN YOU WILL *SUFFER*!" Ogun bellowed into his face. "All of you will suffer until I have what I want."

Aristil's lined face twisted into fury. "You were my greatest failure, Ogun," she snarled, "but the day I expelled you was the happiest day I ever spent as headmistress of Hyperspace High. You are no better than a beast."

The warlord grabbed three of her arms, his talon digging into flesh until she yelped. "You will regret those words." He smiled down at her – a sight that chilled John's blood even more than the roaring and bellowing. With a flick of his wrist, he flung her against the side of a hoverbus. "Get in!" he commanded. "*You* will open the Library of Kerallin for me. It will be *you* who gives Ogun the keys to the universe's knowledge."

Aristil staggered upright, clutching her bruised side. "No, you can't—"

Ogun barked an order. Instantly, the soldier droids raised their weapons, pointing laser rifles into the crowd of scholars. "Get into the hoverbus," the warlord said. "Or your friends will pay the price."

Tears streamed down Aristil's face as she climbed into the hoverbus. "Help us," she wept. "Oh, please help us."

"There is no one here to help you," Ogun sneered, as he climbed in beside her. "Now, take me to your library unless you wish to taste Ogun's anger." Turning back to the droids, he yelled, "Alpha platoon, come with me! Beta platoon, escort the scholars to the hall of assembly. Keep them there until we're ready to leave."

Fifteen soldier droids climbed into the hoverbus. With shaking hands, Aristil leaned forward and touched the controls. The craft turned and flashed across the meadow.

Inside the pyramid, John gazed at a sea of shocked, angry faces. "I've seen enough," he said. "Let's deal with the droids first, and then we'll go after Ogun."

CHAPTER 10

As the soldier droids began pushing scholars towards the remaining hoverbus, John saw Deem pull his fist back for a blow. Socrat clutched at his arm before the Derrilian could throw the punch. Even so, the closest droid smashed Deem in the chest with the butt of its laser rifle. "Resistance will be met with extreme force," it droned.

"I'll show you extreme force," growled the Scholar, lunging forward.

"No, Deem, you'll only make things worse," Socrat panted, hanging onto the Derrilian's arm. "Use your logic. There are too many of them. Get on the hoverbus."

Metal legs clanked as the droids moved forward again, herding the terrified scholars like sheep.

John lifted his hand – the signal to advance. Without looking back, he sprinted through the open portal of Kerallin's pyramid ship. Sixteen students followed on the ground. Spreading his wings, Kaal took to the sky.

Keeping his eyes fixed on the fifteen soldier droids, John's mind worked furiously. *Don't turn around. Please don't turn around*, he repeated to himself over and over, as his heart pumped pure adrenalin. Keeping low and silent, he pounded across the meadow.

John's wishes were answered. None of the droids turned. None saw the attack coming. John screamed, "NOW!" Still yelling, he launched a flying kick. His foot smashed into a droid's metal back in a roundhouse kick, hurling it forward to crash face-first into the grass. Instantly, it tried to rise. John threw himself onto the robot's back, trying to keep it pinned to the ground.

Beneath him, metal shifted.

It began to rise.

Kaal's instructions came back to him in a flash: "Grab any wires you see and rip them out."

As the robot struggled to get up, John spotted a

gap where its head was connected to its neck. Inside was a thick bundle of wires. Reaching down, he grabbed at them.

John pulled with all his strength. Sparks flew. With a fizzing noise, the robot thrashed, almost spearing John on its spiked armour. Then, its power spent, it collapsed.

"One down!" John shouted. Around him chaos had broken out. Several droids had been toppled in the first wave of the attack. As John watched, Raytanna reached out and disconnected a droid's energy conduits with expert fingers. It slumped.

Kaal's tactic was ruthlessly efficient. Wings powering him down from the sky, he took a droid by the head and swooped upward again, the struggling robot dangling beneath him. A hundred metres in the air, he let go. The robot's arms beat at the air for a moment, as if it were trying to fly, then it smashed into the ground, its body wrecked beyond any repair.

By now, though, the droids had had time to organize against the sudden assault. As John watched, the remaining robots fell back into a defensive line. Tossing Queelin to one side like a rag, one more droid rose to its feet and joined the line.

Laser rifles levelled at the students.

John felt his stomach sink. The attack had failed. The students had no chance against laser fire.

"LOOK OUT!"

John's jaw dropped open, as a hoverbus zoomed across the grass and slammed into the line of droids, sending metal bodies sprawling.

Behind the controls, Lishtig punched the air.

A ragged cheer went up from the students and the scholars in the bus. The students threw themselves back into the fight, and Lishtig whipped the hoverbus round, slamming it into a dented droid that was trying to get to its feet. As he drove away, Lishtig whooped, his purple ponytail streaming behind him.

Quickly, John counted the broken droids. Listhig had taken out three.

Only nine left.

"John, help!" A few metres away, Kritta rolled away from a blast of red laser fire.

John hit the attacking droid from behind before it could fire again. Instantly, a metal hand gripped his wrist with unbelievable strength. Feeling as though his arm would break, he shouted in agony.

From the corner of his eye, John caught a blur of motion. With an elegant backflip, Emmie suddenly rose in front of the droid, her fists smashing into its face.

Forced to defend itself, the droid released John's arm and threw itself at its new opponent. But Emmie was too quick. Metal hands grabbed at thin air as she cartwheeled to one side.

The distraction was all John needed. His fingers found bare wires. He yanked, feeling grim satisfaction as sparks fountained and the twitching droid fell.

Eight. Quickly, John rose to his knees, yelling, "Thanks, Emmie!"

"You can owe me dinner at Seefood!" the Silaran girlshouted back, breathing heavily as she dropped into a crouch and sprung at another droid.

John glanced around, looking to see if any of his classmates needed help. Emmie was now helping Kritta fight. Even with the desperate battle raging all around, John couldn't help but admire the way the Silaran girl moved with effortless grace.

More laser fire hissed through the air, narrowly

missing Raytanna, who ducked behind the remaining hoverbus. A droid began walking towards her. Picking up a fallen rifle, John pulled the trigger. A laser beam hit the droid full in the back. John expected the droid to fall, but nothing happened. It carried on pacing towards Raytanna.

The gun must be broken.

The droid was almost on Raytanna now, shouldering its rifle again as it stalked around the hoverbus.

"Noooo!" Turning the weapon in his hands, John ran forward, swinging it like a baseball bat and smashing it into the machine's head.

It turned, bringing its own rifle up to aim at John.

He dived to one side as it fired. A red beam flashed past his head. John crawled backward, fingers clutching at the grass. The droid was already taking aim again. As its metal finger tightened on the trigger, John squeezed his eyes closed.

A second passed. Two.

John opened his eyes.

The droid had stopped. It was standing like a statue with its rifle pointing at John's heart.

He blinked as Raytanna stepped out from behind it.

"Every robot has an off switch," she said.

John scrambled to his feet, looking around quickly. Five droids remained, each armed with a deadly laser rifle. Now, however, the scholars were fighting back as well. With robes flapping, Silva launched himself over the side of the hoverbus, metal clashing on metal, as his own fists lashed out at a droid that was threatening to overwhelm Werril. Following Kaal's example, Deem was lifting another into the sky. Not as quickly as Kaal, John noticed. In old age, the scholar's wings had lost their strength.

Dodging past Kaal and Emmie, John threw himself at a droid that was attacking Queelin. She had managed to disarm it and was fighting with grim intensity, but her arm was hanging uselessly by her side. She ducked as the machine swung a crushing metal fist at her head.

"Gobi!" John shouted. "Catch this."

The droid stumbled to one side as John's body slammed into it – straight into Gobi's massive fist. The huge punch shattered armour. The robot jerked twice and was still.

"John! Look out!"

John whirled at Emmie's shout. One of the droids he had thought was finished had climbed to its feet behind him. Horror clutched his stomach as he found himself staring down the barrel of laser rifle again.

A green thunderbolt dropped from the sky. Kaal descended on the robot in a flurry of flapping wings and smashing fists. The laser rifle spun away. Staggering under the weight of its attacker, the droid fought back. Kaal yelled in pain as its fist crunched into his jaw. The droid twisted and a spike found its mark, tearing through Kaal's uniform and gouging the flesh beneath. Blue blood dripped from the wound, as the Derrilian clutched the droid's head. Kaal shrieked a battle cry. Muscles heaving, he twisted with all his might. With a crack and a shower of sparks, the soldier droid's head came away from its body.

Kaal threw it to one side. "Remind me to use that move in Boxogle," he said, winking at John.

"Help! Help me!" John and Kaal both spun this time. Close to the banks of a stream, Mordant Talliver was caught in a droid's embrace, a metal hand reaching for his throat.

CHAPTER 11

The half-Gargon was thrashing at the robot with long black tentacles, but his blows were wildly random. Rather than damaging the droid, he was in danger of wounding himself on its spikes.

"Stop your attack," the machine droned.

Behind it, Emmie hesitated. A look crossed her face. John knew exactly what she was thinking – *why help Mordant Talliver?* For a moment their eyes met. Emmie lifted her eyebrows in an unspoken question: *Well?*

John stared at her, his mind like a rollercoaster. Mordant had never lifted a finger to help anyone but himself. He went out of his way to insult and bully anyone who crossed his path. Yet, for all that he would never be a friend, he was a Hyperspace High student. They owed him their help.

John's head moved in a tiny nod.

Muscles in his legs tensed to run forward. Emmie leapt into the air, lashing out with a kick that staggered the droid straight into John and Kaal. Mordant screamed as both of them leapt at the same moment, crashing into the machine. "Into the water!" John shouted, heaving with all his might.

The droid released Mordant as it lurched backward. For a second, it tottered on the muddy bank of the stream and then it fell. Water hissed and fizzled. The robot tried to rise, clawing its way to the bank. Then its power source exploded. Lifeless metal remains fell backward.

"It took you long enough," Mordant choked out. He pushed himself to his knees, hands rubbing red skin around his neck.

"Don't mention it," said John sarcastically. "Always happy to help."

"If you're expecting thanks, you won't get it from

me. If it wasn't for you, we'd be halfway back to Hyperspace High by now."

Ignoring Mordant's complaints, John turned to look for another droid to attack. The fight was now all but over. Lishtig was beating at one droid with the mangled remains of its own arm. A few metres away, Gobi held the last robot in a tight hug. The spikes on its armour meant nothing to him. They bent and snapped as Gobi's massive arms squeezed tighter and tighter. Metal squealed and buckled; electronic circuits exploded.

"Never pick a fight with a Koo-rag-tar," growled Gobi, as he dropped the droid into a crumpled heap of scrap metal at his feet.

"Is anyone hurt?" John yelled. Seeing that all the Hyperspace High students were on their feet, he breathed a sigh of relief. But a few of his classmates were bleeding, and Queelin's arm was bent at a strange angle.

By the time John got to her, Bareon was already there, making soothing noises as he bent over her arm, his fingers brushing her jet-black skin lightly. Her arm was obviously broken, though she was trying not to let the pain show on her face.

"I'll be OK to help finish Ogun off," she hissed through clenched teeth.

Bareon looked up sharply. "You'll do no more fighting today," he said briskly. "Raytanna and Werril, that goes for you, too. I want to see to those wounds." Turning to John, he finished quietly, "I don't suppose you're going to let me look at this, are you?" He brushed John's cheek with a long, grey finger and held it up before John's eyes.

Blood dripped. "I ... uh ... didn't know," John said. "Is it bad?"

"Take two minutes to fix it in a proper medical facility," Bareon shrugged. "Until then, it will start throbbing soon, but – don't worry – you'll live."

"Good," said John. "Now, it's Ogun's turn."

"He took Aristil to the library. We'll fight with you," interrupted Deem, landing a few metres away. Silva and Thushlar came to stand beside him. John couldn't help noticing that the old Derrilian was sweating heavily, his breath coming in short, painful pants. The scholars were old, he reminded himself. Their fighting days were long behind them.

"I've got a better idea," he said quickly. "You know Kerallin better than us. Take care of the wounded and send a distress signal. Alert Hyperspace High and the Galactic Council. The rest of us will take care of Ogun."

John glanced back at his classmates, seeing determination in their faces. Only Mordant Talliver was standing to one side, a sulky look on his face.

Reaching up, Thushlar slapped him on the back, beaming at the other scholars. "Ha!" he cackled. "I like this one. I told you, didn't I? We should get more of these human Earthlings into Hyperspace High."

"It's no good," panted Gobi-san-Art. He and Kaal had their shoulders braced against the library doors and were heaving with all their combined strength. "It's in lock-down. We'd need a guided missile to get through."

"Is there any other way in?" Lishtig asked impatiently.

"The retina scan opens the doors," said Emmie, nodding towards a small box hidden in the shadows by the door. "But it won't recognize any of us. If we asked one of the scholars to activate it—"

"I don't think that's a good idea, Emmie," John interrupted. "Let's keep the scholars as far from danger as we can."

"Maybe I can hack it," said Kaal. Leaning over, he took from his pocket the ToTool he always carried with him. John always thought of the small device as a space-age Swiss Army knife. It seemed to be able to transform into any tool Kaal needed at the touch of a small button. Now, a spike that looked like a very fine screwdriver flicked out of the slim, silver device. Within seconds, Kaal had removed the front of the retina scanner, revealing complex circuits within.

"How long will it take?" John asked.

"It will take as long as it takes," Kaal replied. "We're not getting in any other way. Unless you have a guided missile on you."

John folded his arms nervously.

The Derrilian muttered under his breath as he worked: "Bypass the optic recognition programme ... patch the locking circuits to the main board ... delete the input codes ... input command ..."

From the door came the sound of internal bolts

snapping into a new position.

"Quick enough for you?" asked Kaal, standing.

The door swung open silently.

Inside, soldier droids were busy emptying shelves and packing globes into foam-lined trays. At the centre of the library, and surrounded by the shining worlds the students had left in place, stood Ogun. Aristil was tied securely to a MorphSeat, a gag across her mouth.

"Faster, you walking junkyards!" the warlord roared. "Work faster, or I'll have you all melted down."

Behind him, a droid dropped a globe. It smashed to the ground, a slick of thick liquid spreading across the floor.

The warlord cursed. Crossing to the droid he bent over it, flames streaming from his nostrils, and swung a massive punch that threw the droid across the library. "Be *CAREFUL*!" Ogun bellowed. "I might have wished to invade that world. Because of your clumsiness, it is now lost to me."

Its visor blackened with soot, the droid clattered to its feet and backed away.

"STOP!" John flung open the library doors,

flooding the room with sunlight. Behind him stood the students of Hyperspace High.

Ogun turned, blinking in the sudden sunlight. "What the—"

John gave him no time to finish. He walked towards the centre of the library, hands held behind his back so that the warlord would not see them trembling. Hoping his voice did not betray his fear, he said coolly, "Beta platoon has been defeated, Ogun. Right now, the scholars are contacting Hyperspace High and the Galactic Council. There will be a fleet of ships here any moment. Go now and you might just escape, though I wouldn't bet on it."

"And *who* are *YOU*?" Ogun demanded, striding forward to meet John halfway down a row of shelves.

John thought he could feel the floor shaking as the towering warlord stepped towards him. He looked up into eyes that glinted with vicious madness. Wisps of flame licked around the red scales of Ogun's face.

Keeping his voice steady, John said, "I am—"

Ogun's taloned hand reached out and grabbed John's uniform top. John's feet left the floor as the warlord lifted him, glaring down at the logo printed on his uniform. "You are a Hyperspace High student," he spat, throwing John to one side.

John slammed into a row of shelves, falling to his knees. Forcing himself to stand upright on shaking legs, he tried to speak again. "Yes—"

Ogun cut him off. "I thought you had already left Kerallin," he hissed. "But it makes no difference to my plans. You will join the scholars as my hostages."

Words died in John's mouth, as the warlord looked over the classmates scornfully. Silently, he cursed himself. Maybe this time Mordant had been right. Maybe it *was* madness to face this huge warlord.

"Hyperspace High," Ogun continued, "it's the greatest school in the universe, isn't it?"

His question was met by silence.

"You probably think you're all so very clever."

Once again, his words were met by blank faces.

The warlord's eyes blazed with contempt. "Well, I, too, was once a student at Hyperspace High," he growled, taking a step closer and glaring at the students one by one. "It's a school for the weak. A school for those who will never have the strength to grasp glory in their hands." A talon poked Kaal in the chest, forcing the muscular Derrilian backward.

Ogun snorted flame. "Pathetic," he said. "Look at you all. None of you fit to kiss my boots. But you are not to blame. You are only what your precious school has made you."

"That's not—" Listhtig began.

"SILENCE!" roared Ogun, fire pouring from his snout. "You will speak when I tell you to speak."

John flinched. Danger sparked in Ogun's eyes. A moment later the warlord chuckled, his laughter sounding even more insane than his fury. "Being expelled from Hyperspace High was the making of me," he said. "Free of petty rules and useless classes, I began my rise to greatness. I fought for years to become the leader of my people, and when I had achieved that, I began long years of conquest. Now, six worlds bow to me. More will soon follow."

Finally, John found his voice. "No, you'll be blasted to pieces trying to escape Kerallin," he said quietly.

"I SAID, *SILENCE*." Ogun turned on John. "How long do you think it will take the Galactic Council to get their war fleet here? And even if they arrive in time to catch me, do you think they will fire on a ship carrying the scholars of Kerallin and students as hostages?"

John's jaw dropped open.

"I see you did not consider those details," Ogun laughed. "Which is why you will never be as great as me." He paused for a moment, a talon scratching the scales on his chin. "And yet, and yet ... you may be of some use."

Again, he scanned the student's faces. "It is true that Hyperspace High takes only the best of students from every solar system. Perhaps if you forget everything you learned there and joined with me, I could still make something of you. In years to come you might make useful lieutenants and generals. Maybe I will give you your own planets to rule. In my name, of course."

Ogun threw his head back and bellowed with laughter. "Yes," he said when his laugher had died. "I will make you all an offer – come with me and you will never have to go to school again." He waved a talon at the globes above. "You can still be masters of all the knowledge in the universe. What have you got to lose? Especially as I will kill anyone who refuses."

Kaal stepped forward, scowling. "You're mad," he growled. "None of us would ever join you."

"Mad, am I?" Flames flared from Ogun's snout as he rounded on Kaal. "What planet are you from?"

"Derril," Kaal answered quickly, his eyes darting towards the globe he had left in the centre of the library. It hadn't yet been packed by the droids, who continued gathering up the globes. "Where we believe that all people and all knowledge should be free."

"Oh, is that what you believe?" Ogun said, smirking. A talon stretched out, pointing to the globe that Kaal had glanced at. The warlord snapped an order and a droid brought it to him.

Kaal faced him, anger in his eyes as Ogun tossed the globe into the air.

"All the knowledge of Derril," the warlord chuckled. "Shall I use it to conquer the planet? Or shall I smash it as I will soon smash you?" Carelessly, he threw the globe upward once more.

"You leave Derril *alone*," snarled Kaal. With a flick of his wings, he lunged into the air and snatched the globe before Ogun could catch it.

"How dare you defy me!" howled the warlord. Fire roaring around his head, he threw himself at Kaal.

With a snap of his wings, Kaal dodged to one side. "Queelin!" Kaal called, throwing the globe.

Queelin leapt, catching the glowing ball with easy grace.

Kaal forgotten, Ogun turned on her. "Give it to me," he roared, "or suffer the penalty for your disobedience."

"Gobi, catch!" yelled Queelin, as talons stretched towards her.

Once again the globe spun through the air. This time Gobi-san-Art's thick fingers curled around it.

"John!" Gobi shouted, sending the globe past Ogun's fiery head, as the warlord wheeled around.

John caught it. "To you, Lishtig!" he called as the warlord spun round. He heaved the ball upward.

With a yell of triumph, the warlord jumped, heavily muscled legs pushing him upward in an impossible leap. "Mine," he grunted, as his talons closed around the globe.

For a moment, he glared at the students as if daring them to try and take the world again. Then, he sniggered. Staring Kaal in the face, he stretched out a hand and let the globe drop.

Kaal hurled himself forward. "*Nooo!*" he yelled, as he dived. Too late. The globe smashed on the marble floor.

John looked down in horror as a million sparkling shards tinkled to the floor and a thick, multi-coloured liquid swirled briefly around Kaal's knees before evaporating into nothing.

The Derrilian looked up, tears in his eyes.

"Not so clever now, eh?" said Ogun.

With a cry of pure hatred, Kaal got to his feet and charged, fists raised to pound the warlord's face.

A plume of fire sent him staggering back. "Who wants their planet to be next?" Ogun roared, flames flickering around his face.

No one spoke. Wide-eyed, the students took a step backward.

"Good," Ogun said, grinning. "On this one occasion, I will overlook your disobedience as youthful high spirits." His grin turned to a growl. "*If* you join with me. I have no more time to play games with children, so make your decisions now."

Emmie stepped forward, her face stern.

John's mind whirled. *She's going to attack him. He'll kill her.*

"Don't, Emmie! Get back!" he shouted, reaching out to pull her away from the insane warlord.

Emmie pushed his hand away. Ignoring John, she looked up into Ogun's face. "I will come with you," she said.

CHAPTER 12

John blinked. Seconds slipped by. He tried to speak. Nothing came out of his mouth but a choking noise. "Emmie ... Emmie – you can't do this," he finally managed to gasp.

"Please, Emmie, no," Kaal echoed. "What about your friends? What about us?"

Behind him, shocked murmurs ran through the students.

"Is she serious?" John heard Lishtig groan, "Why does she want to go off with that waste of molecules?"

"Beats me," Gobi-san-Art replied, shaking his head. "I always thought Emmie Tarz was, you know, pretty cool."

"Well, I'm not at all surprised," Mordant Talliver interrupted in a whisper loud enough for everyone to hear. "Why would the stupidest girl in school want to stay? She made a complete mess of the inspection, too. Dropping out before she's thrown out is probably the cleverest thing she's ever done."

John fought down an urge to turn round and punch the black-haired boy. Instead, he glanced at Kaal. The Derrilian's face was frozen in horror. As if the destruction of his planet's knowledge wasn't bad enough, his friend had just betrayed them. John guessed at how he must feel. Like his world was crumbling around him. He had always admired the Silaran girl's strength and courage. Even though he'd only known her for a handful of weeks, he couldn't begin to imagine life without her. It just didn't seem possible that Emmie would walk away from Hyperspace High, and all her friends, so easily.

"Emmie," he choked again, reaching towards her. "Don't go."

His friend didn't seem to hear. She ran a hand through her silvery hair, hooking a wayward strand behind a pointed ear. Then she smiled up at Ogun. "I just realized in the last few minutes," she said, "I'm useless at learning and sick of coming bottom of every class. Every day I try my best, and every day I do worse than before. Why should I spend years feeling like a failure when I could help conquer the universe with a great warlord?"

John's heart sank further. He had known that Emmie struggled with most of her classes, but never guessed that she was so unhappy. *Why didn't she say something? Kaal and I could have helped.*

John watched miserably as Ogun smiled down at Emmie. "You are wise beyond learning," the warlord said. "At my side you will rise to greatness and glory above anything Hyperspace High could offer."

"Thank you, Master Ogun," said Emmie. "I may not be a good student, but I am an excellent pilot."

"Then perhaps one day you shall command my fleet."

Emmie bowed her head. "It would be an honour."

"Your classmates would do well to follow your example," Ogun continued, staring around. "Who else will join this wise young Silaran? Who else will follow me and write their name across history?"

Lishtig was the first to speak. "I wouldn't follow you anywhere," he snorted.

"That's right!" spat John. "Emmie can do what she likes, but I would *never* join up with a thug like you."

"That goes for me, too," said Kaal. "I'd rather die."

"And very soon, you *will*!" roared Ogun, flames of anger spouting from his nostrils once more. "Until then, you will watch as the knowledge of Kerallin falls into my grasp." The warlord turned away. "Move the scholars onto my ship," he commanded, pointing at four of the droids. "The rest of you continue your packing. I will *personally* ensure that these children do not escape."

As four soldier droids clanked through the library doors, Ogun gripped Emmie's shoulder. "Your first task will be to help pack up this library," he said. "And then we will load the globes onto my ship."

"Certainly, Master Ogun," said Emmie, bobbing her head again. "After the test the scholars put me through earlier, it will be a pleasure to steal their globes."

The warlord roared with laughter, as Emmie climbed

a row of shelves and began throwing planets into his waiting hands.

"You and I are going to get on famously!" he called up to her. "The half-Gargon boy thinks you're stupid, but they said that about me when I was at Hyperspace High. We will show them how stupid we are when we rule the skies."

Emmie threw more globes. Ogun caught them, gently placing each into a packing crate. "No one could say you are stupid, Master Ogun," she said. "Robbing the Library of Kerallin is a stroke of genius. They say that knowledge is power. If that's true, you'll become the most powerful being in the universe in one stroke."

"None but me would dare hatch such a plan," replied the warlord. "It is good that you see the simple brilliance of it."

"You're right, Master Ogun. At Hyperspace High the teachers make everything so *complicated*. Real genius is always simple."

John frowned. Why was Emmie talking like this? Fawning over Ogun, his friend sounded exactly like Mordant's Serve-U-Droid, G-Vez.

As if reading his thoughts, Kaal quietly stepped closer. "What's she doing?" he whispered in John's ear.

"I don't know," John whispered back. "I've never seen her act like this before."

"It doesn't change anything. We still have to stop Ogun. Afterward maybe we can talk to Emmie. Make her see there's still a place for her at Hyperspace High."

John nodded his head slightly. "You're right, this isn't over yet." Carefully, he looked around. Emmie and Ogun were emptying shelves rapidly. Further away, the remaining six soldier droids were doing the same. Hundreds of planets had already been boxed, waiting to be taken to Ogun's warship.

"We could take out the droids," John said from the corner of his mouth.

"Too dangerous," Kaal replied. "How many globes will get broken if we start fighting in here? Plus, we'd still have *him* to deal with." He nodded at Ogun.

"And Emmie, too," John whispered sadly. "I don't want to fight Emmie."

"If we can get out of the library, we could sabotage

Ogun's ship, take the scholars, and fly the pyramid into orbit. If they managed to get a message out to Hyperspace High, the Galactic Council fleet will be on the way. Ogun will be stuck here until they arrive."

John bit his lip thoughtfully. He had to admit that Kaal's was a good plan, even if the idea of leaving Emmie behind horrified him.

She's made her choice. If Ogun gets away, the entire galaxy might fall. How long until he gets to Earth?

"OK," he whispered. "Let's do it. Put the word out."

John's eyes remained fixed on Ogun, as Kaal leant over behind him and whispered instructions in Lishtig's ear. In turn, Lishtig whispered to Gobi, who passed the message on to Mordant.

Within a few minutes, Kaal leaned forward. "Ready," he hissed. "We'll go slow. Run for it if he sees us."

Without replying, John began moving silently towards the door. Risking a look away from the warlord, he glanced at the exit.

Miles away.

Quickly, he returned his gaze to Ogun. The warlord

was busy, placing globe after globe into crates while boasting of his exploits to Emmie.

"On Jaheera-Six, we faced an army of 200,000," he said, chuckling. "They quickly fell to my forces. I took the rest of the planet within days and destroyed every one of their capital cities as a punishment."

John took another step. Then another. Slowly, quietly, the small group of students was moving towards the door.

Emmie looked down. "Forgive me, Master Ogun," she said, sounding slightly ashamed. "I can't quite reach the next shelf. Could you give me a boost?"

"By my hands, you will be lifted to ever greater heights. Why not begin now?" Chuckling, the warlord reached up a taloned hand for Emmie to step into.

Instead, her hand gripped his wrist. In a breathtakingly fast blur of movement, Emmie swung down, using her own momentum to twist the warlord's arm up behind his back.

"If you think I would ever abandon Hyperspace High for *you*, you really are stupid!" she yelled in the warlord's ear, pulling his arm up with a creak of bones.

"Fool! I will kill you for this!" Ogun bellowed, his

voice a mixture of pain and fury. "You will die. You will all *die.*" A sheet of flame billowed from his scaled snout, pouring onto the shelves. The fire caught, spreading along the shelves. One by one, globes shattered in the heat.

In the centre of the fire, Emmie clung to Ogun's arm, twisting his arm higher up his back, her face a mask of anger. "I learnt this move in Plutonian Karate lessons at Hyperspace High!" she shouted. "Looks like not everything they teach there is useless."

"Get off me, you miserable traitor!" roared Ogun, heaving beneath her, plunging dangerously close to the flames.

Emmie jerked his arm up another few centimetres, making the enraged warlord squeal in agony. "On your knees or I'll break it," she commanded.

"I will never surrender to a *child.*"

For a few seconds, John and the rest of the class were frozen, stunned by the ferocity of Emmie's whirlwind attack. Now, they leapt forward to help, coughing and choking on the thick smoke engulfing the library.

Kaal's foot lashed out, cutting Ogun's legs from

beneath him. The warlord slammed face-down on the floor with an "*Oof!*" as air was forced out of his lungs. Still, Emmie gripped his arm, her legs either side of his broad back.

John jumped, adding his weight to Emmie's and pinning the warlord's body to the ground. "Good to have you back, Emmie!" he yelled. "I really thought we'd lost you for a moment there."

"As if!" Emmie yelled back. Looking down at Ogun, she shouted, "Will you just keep *still,* you space thug!"

On either side of them, Lishtig and Gobi-san-Art leapt past the thrashing, bucking figure on the marble floor. Dodging flames and yelling, "Hyperspace High!" they launched themselves at two soldier droids that were rushing to help their master. With a crash, both went down. Through the smoke, John heard more fighting as the students moved into the library to deal with the rest of the droids.

"Idiot children!" the warlord screeched. "Even if you defeat me, the Library of Kerallin will burn. All the scholars' knowledge will be lost." With another roar, more flames belched from his snout. Another shelf caught fire.

Coughing, John looked around. Ogun was right: the library was rapidly turning into an inferno. Already, the smoke was making it difficult to breathe. Within a few minutes, it would mean death to remain inside. Higher up the shelves, globes shattered, sounding like gunshots and raining splinters of glass. Further along the shelves, he could hear more shouting. For a split second he remembered Professor Raydon's class, wishing he could flick a zero-gravity switch. The deafening noise would soon put the fire out.

Pushing the thought out of his head, he bellowed, "We have to get out of here, Emmie!" over the roar of fire. "The library's lost."

Emmie looked up at him, her face lined with the strain of keeping Ogun locked in the Plutonian Karate hold. Her navy-blue eyes reflected dancing flames. "No," she said. "It's not lost yet. Use the Earth, John."

CHAPTER 13

Through thickening smoke, John stared at Emmie blankly.

The Silaran girl shifted her weight, pushing Ogun's arm higher up his back. "Remember what you said about Earth in Space Survival class," she said urgently as the warlord cursed her. "About putting out fires." She twisted Ogun's arm, hissing, "Keep still, you intergalactic slimeball!"

In a flash, John understood. "What about you?" he asked, glancing around at the raging fire. "Will you be OK?"

Emmie nodded. "I don't know for how long,

though. You need to be fast." She coughed as fresh smoke billowed. *"Go."*

The smoke thickened by the second, as the shelves became walls of fire. John hesitated. He hated leaving Emmie to deal with the huge warrior on her own, but the rest of the class was fighting droids. He had no choice.

Falling to his hands and knees, John crawled back towards the centre of the library, where he had last seen the Earth globe. Flames licked the shelves to either side of him. Smoke stung his eyes and throat: the blaze was burning brighter by the second. After a few metres he looked back over his shoulder. Emmie had already disappeared behind a wall of smoke. Hearing her cough, he forced himself to move faster.

Another two metres.

To one side, a broken soldier droid reached out to clutch at his ankle with a metal hand. John kicked it away, thanking his lucky stars that Gobi had crushed the machine so badly, it couldn't move. Over the roar of flames he could hear the sounds of fighting further into the library. There was no time to wonder who was winning, though.

Keeping close to the ground where the air was slightly less thick with smoke, John crawled on. Flames bloomed around him. He could feel his hair crisping, heat beginning to scorch the skin on his face.

Ten metres from where John had left Emmie, the smoke cleared a little. John looked around as he rose to his feet. There was no sign of his classmates, but he could hear shouting as they fought Ogun's soldier droids in a distant part of the library. So far the fire had only taken hold of a part of the library, but it was spreading rapidly.

There's no time. I'm too late.

John paused. Part of his brain was frantically telling him to run back to Emmie, to drag her away from danger. He stopped himself. Emmie wasn't the only one whose life was at risk. If the blazing shelves at the entrance to the library collapsed, all the students would be trapped inside. Covering his mouth and nose with one hand, he sprinted through smoke. He skidded to a halt as he got to the centre of the library, spinning around in horror.

The Earth had gone.

So, too, had Silar, Gargon ... all the students' home

planets had been packed up. John looked around desperately, hands balled into fists, sweat dripping down his forehead. A few packing crates lay open close by. He checked them. All were empty. Panic rising, John tore the gag from Aristil's mouth and started untying her.

"Leave me," the old scholar gasped. "There's no time."

"I need the Earth," John told her.

"That way." Aristil nodded towards an aisle. "Row twenty-three. A droid took all the planets."

Following her gaze, John saw a soldier droid through wisps of smoke. Following its master's orders, it was carrying globes to a crate as if nothing was happening in the library. In its hands was a familiar blue planet.

"JOHN, *HURRY!*" Emmie's shout ended in a hacking cough.

There was no time for hesitation. He raced towards the droid, throwing himself into a flying kick. Warned of his approach by Emmie's shout, the droid turned and swiftly dodged away. John sailed past, landing in a crouch.

He glared up at the robot. "Your master is defeated.

Give me the globe."

"You will surrender. Any attempts to escape will be met with extreme force," the droid droned.

Cursing under his breath, John launched himself at the droid once more, hands reaching out for the wires at its neck.

Transferring the globe to one hand, the robot smashed a metal fist towards him. John tried to turn aside but the blow grazed his cheek, reopening the cut another droid had given him earlier. Blood dripped from his chin. Wiping it away with the back of his hand, he circled.

"You will surrender."

"I will *not*." Dropping, John lashed out with his foot again.

The droid clanked backward.

One last chance, John told himself. Lifting his head, he yelled. "*KAAL!*" with all the strength in his lungs. "Get in the air. Catch this!"

With a massive surge of energy, he threw himself at the droid again. It dodged to avoid the blow, but misjudged John's target. This time John wasn't aiming for the droid itself, but for the globe in its hand.

Striking like a football player, John caught the Earth globe on his foot, launching it straight up into the air. The droid spun round angrily, unsure how to respond to this new attack. John ignored it. He was already running backward as he landed, his eyes following the globe as it flew upward, up towards the top of the shelves. Then it stopped and began to drop.

On thrashing wings, Kaal rocketed into the air.

"YES. GO ON, KAAL!"

Green hands reached out and held the globe. And like a goalkeeper, Kaal hugged it to his chest, hanging in the air on flapping wings.

John ran back towards the flames, back towards Emmie. "TO ME!" he bellowed over his shoulder.

Kaal darted forward, soaring over John's head and dropping the globe into his friend's outstretched hands.

"Too small," John muttered to himself as his hand moved across the surface. Instantly, the globe grew to the size of a large beach ball. "Still not enough." He passed his hand over it again, lifting the swirling globe above his head to balance it. Now continents could be seen clearly, rippled with mountain ranges.

Clouds swirled beneath his hands. He made it larger still.

"*HURRY, JOHN!*" In the centre of the blazing inferno, Emmie screamed.

"I'm coming, Emmie!" he shouted back. Keeping the enormous ball balanced on one hand, he looked up. Beneath his fingers was the map of Britain. Quickly, John tapped on the Pacific Ocean, focusing in on it until the ocean's grey waters filled the globe. Taking two steps, he flung the huge sphere with all his strength. The massive ball spun in the air for a moment.

"I hope you're right about this, Emmie!" John shouted, as he watched it fall.

With a crash that shook the ground, the Earth shattered at the centre of the flames. Water flooded from its broken shell in a tsunami-like crash. The Thames emptied in a rushing wave that smashed along the shelves, drowning the fire and smashing the few globes that remained. John braced himself as the wave swept towards him.

The torrent of water swept him off his feet, pulling him underwater. Another shelf stopped him

– painfully. Clambering to his feet, John strained forward to remain upright, as the water dropped to chest height, then waist height. Great clouds of steam hissed upward, creating a thick, hot mist. The damage was terrible. As the water settled into an knee-deep pool and the mist cleared, John saw ruined empty shelves, blackened by fire and now dripping wet.

"*EMMIE!*" he spluttered, coughing water as his senses returned in a rush. Splashing forward, he found her huddled at the centre of the wreckage. With one hand, she still held grimly onto the unconscious warlord's arm. Her wet uniform clung to her; her hair hung in soaked strands over her face.

"Emmie. Are you OK?" John panted, grabbing her shoulder.

Emmie lifted her head. With her free hand, she brushed hair out of her eyes. "Like I said, you're lucky to live on a planet with so much water," she said, grinning.

"That was a brilliant idea!" John shouted. You are brilliant, Emmie. *Brilliant*!"

"You weren't bad, either," she told him. "A bit slow on the uptake, but not bad."

Around them the water was rapidly disappearing. Like the other smashed globes, the contents of the Earth had become a thick multi-coloured liquid before evaporating into nothing.

Beneath Emmie's knees, Ogun stirred. "What?" he croaked in a dazed voice. "What's happening?"

"You're finished is what's happening," John replied, furiously. "Thanks to Emmie, the fire's out. You'll be staying right here while we wait for the Galactic Council fleet to arrive. I'm guessing there's a prison cell somewhere with your name on the door."

"Never. The Galactic fleet will never take me alive." The warlord began struggling. John dropped, quickly twisting Ogun's other arm up his back.

"Curse you!" shrieked the warlord. "I am Ogun, emperor of six worlds. I will *never* be defeated." He snorted, trying to breathe fire. A few pathetic puffs of steam trailed from his damp nostrils.

John and Emmie looked at each other.

"I don't know about you, Emmie," John said, "But I can't believe I ever thought this guy was terrifying." He added, "Plus, I've got a feeling he might be wrong about the whole never-be-defeated thing."

Emmie nodded. "Yeah, from where I'm sitting – which is on his back holding him in an armlock – he looks *totally* defeated."

A few metres away a droid crashed to the ground, sparks hissing from its ripped armour. "Sorry about that," Gobi said. He nodded at the two of them sitting on Ogun's back. "That looks like fun. Can I have a turn?"

John looked up at the craggy boy, eyes wide. In the excitement of drowning the flames, he had forgotten the rest of the class was still fighting the remaining droids. Relief flooded through him as he saw what was happening further along the row of wrecked shelves. Behind Gobi, Lishtig held a soldier droid in a tight grip from behind, while Mordant ripped out its wires with strong tentacles. Not far from them, Kaal's heavy muscles bulged as he ripped a soldier droid's head from its body.

"That was the last one," Kaal said with satisfaction in his voice, as the metal remains clanked to the ground. "Good work, everyone. That's game and match to Hyperspace Hi—"

The sentence went unfinished. Once more, the sound of a wailing alarm filled the air.

CHAPTER 14

The students looked at each other in horror.

"Oh no. What *now*?" John groaned. The alarm cut off abruptly. Clustering around John and Emmie, as they pinned the helpless warlord, the students looked around nervously.

"Can, I just say," said Lishtig quietly, "if another warlord's landed, this time I'm voting with Mordant."

"Shut up, Lishtig. I can hear something," hissed Emmie. "Something's coming. It sounds like clapping—"

She closed her mouth, as Aristil appeared around the end of the row of shelves. Free of her bonds, the scholar was clapping her six hands together. Hyperspace High's old headmistress no longer looked hunched and bent. She walked tall: ancient, but still full of life and energy. Behind her was the rest of the scholars. They were all applauding. A few at the back began cheering.

John looked around and saw in the faces of his classmates the same confusion he was feeling. Kaal shrugged. "I guess we did save them from the clutches of an evil warlord," he said. "That's probably worth a round of applause."

Beneath John, Ogun shifted position. "Umm ... guys," he said. "This armlock *really* hurts, could you – you know – let go now?"

"We'll let you go when the Galactic fleet gets here," Emmie snapped back. "Do you think we're stupid?"

"It's quite all right," Aristil said. "Emmie, John: please release your prisoner."

"No. Ogun's dangerous."

"Please, Emmie," said Aristil. "We are completely safe. I promise you."

Slowly, John and Emmie let go of the warlord's arms. Standing, they stepped back as Ogun rose to his feet, rubbing his shoulders. He winked at Emmie. "That's quite some grip you have," he said, chuckling.

Confused, John turned to face Aristil and the still-clapping scholars. "What … what's happening here?" he asked.

Socrat moved forward to stand beside Aristil. "A test," he said. "The invasion of Kerallin was a test we created to see how each of you would react in a situation that demanded courage, physical fitness, leadership, teamwork, and applying your knowledge in extreme circumstances." Reaching out, he took Ogun's hand and shook it warmly. "Thank you so much for coming, Ray-ool. It has been a pleasure to see you again after all these years. Your acting skills are a marvel to watch. Amazing. We will have to make use of you again next time if you can find the time."

Emmie looked up at Ogun, bewildered. "You're not a warlord?" she asked.

"Ray-ool Kalaam, at your service," replied "Ogun", bowing with another chuckle. "I'm an actor: star of Oravia's favourite soap opera, *Nebula Zone Twelve*. It's been a pleasure working with you all." Stepping forward, he clapped enormous talons onto John and

Emmie's shoulders. "No hard feelings, I hope."

John fought a sudden urge to break out of the actor's grip and run. Looking up at into the scaled, dragon-like face with its twisted horns and great golden crest, it was difficult to believe he wasn't a fearsome intergalactic warlord. "So, none of it was true?" he gasped.

Ray-ool Kalaam grinned down at him, wisps of smoke curling from his nostrils. "Well, I'm not a warlord, but I *did* go to Hyperspace High," he answered. "I remember my own test very well. The scholars 'accidentally' turned a twenty-metre Danarian Murderbeast loose and we had to recapture it. Of course, it was one of Silva's clever robots, programmed not to actually harm anyone, but we didn't know that. If you thought Ogun was bad, you should try staring down the throat of a howling Murderbeast!"

John looked from the actor, to the scholars, and back again. His jaw moved up and down, but no words came out.

"But we were in real danger," Kaal said, sounding angry. "The droids had guns. Some of us were hurt. Queelin's arm was broken. We could have been killed in the fire!"

"Your classmates have been watching your progress on holo-screen in the canteen," said Aristil softly. "Queelin Temerate was completely healed two minutes after you all left for the library. The lasers were weak, just red light really, though no one was going to notice that in the heat of battle. Meanwhile, we were monitoring the situation closely at all times. If any of you had been in serious danger, the test would have been stopped immediately."

"But ... but ..." stammered Kaal.

"Did you really expect only to answer a few questions and give a presentation?" asked Aristil. "Hyperspace High is the greatest school in the universe. We demand more from you than the ability to repeat what you have learnt in your lessons."

"Thousands of years ago, the scholars found that the only accurate way to assess students was to put them in a situation where they did not know they were being tested. For that reason, and to protect the Scholars' privacy, we ask that you never speak of what happened here."

"Did we pass?" Emmie asked abruptly. "After

putting us through all that, you could at least tell us whether we've passed or not."

Aristil's wrinkled face lit up with a grin. Her eyes glittered. "The results of your test will be given to the headmaster," she said. As the students started to protest, she held up a hand. Her grin widened. "But I think we might be able to give you a clue."

As she finished, the old scholars burst into applause once more. A few cheers turned into a gale. John felt sharp talons digging into his shoulder. He and Emmie looked up at the actor. "Well done," said Ray-ool Kalaam. "I think you passed."

As the cheering subsided, Aristil smiled at Emmie again. "This doesn't mean you can neglect your Hyperspace History studies, though," she said.

Emmie returned her grin. "Fighting Ogun, nearly being burnt alive, and then drowned was *much* easier than your questions," she said. "I'm going to have nightmares about standing on that stage in front of the scholars of Kerallin for a very long time."

"Oh, we're not that bad once you get to know us," laughed Aristil. "Come on, let's find you some clean clothes and get some food inside you." Taking

Emmie's arm, she led her towards the library exit, chatting as if she and Emmie were old friends. John could hear his friend giggling as they walked out into the sunshine.

John looked down to see Thushlar standing beside him. "Professor Dibali, your mathematics teacher, is an old pupil of mine," the scholar said. "Now and then he writes to me. His last two letters have been full of praise for the talents of a certain young Earthling he teaches. I wondered if we might talk?"

John blushed. "Umm …" he stuttered. "Thank you, sir,but I wouldn't want to bother you."

"Tsh," the old scholar wheezed. "We old people love to poke our noses in where they don't belong. And when your nose is as big as mine, it gets a lot of practice."

Laughing, John walked into the bright sunlight with the hunched old scholar cracking jokes alongside him. Glancing behind, he saw that Kaal was already deep in conversation with Deem, Lishtig with a scholar whose skin was made up of multi-coloured patches, and Mordant with Ulara Forshart. As he watched, all the students were swamped by friendly scholars asking eager questions.

Socrat clapped his hands together. "Please!" he shouted in his creaking voice. "The students will be hungry and thirsty. We should continue chatting in the canteen."

Twenty minutes later, John was sitting in a MorphSeat at a long wooden table inside one of the towers. The stone walls were pierced with holes allowing rays of sunlight to flood into the room, lighting vases of flowers from Kerallin's gardens.

With a promise that he would be taking an interest in John's future, Thushlar had reluctantly let go of his arm long enough for John to take a Sonic Shower and change into a fresh uniform. A Meteor Medic had taken care of his cut, dabbing a colourless paste into it with its slender robotic fingers. John ran a hand over his cheek. The skin was smooth, and looked as though it had never been touched.

Scholars walked around the table, putting glasses of goldberry juice and bowls of grey mush in front of each student. Taking a sip of the juice, John looked at the contents of the bowl and wrinkled his nose. After everything that had happened, he had been hoping for something more appetizing, preferably his mum's macaroni cheese.

"Hey, John," Lishtig laughed across the table. "You should have seen your face when Socrat told us the whole attack had been a test. You looked like you'd been hit by a meteorite."

"He wasn't the only one," said Emmie from the seat next to John's. "I never thought for a second that dusty old scholars could be so ... so ... devious and *sneaky*." Looking up, she caught Aristil's eye. "Oh, sorry, I didn't mean to—"

"That's all right, dear," Aristil said with a grin. "I don't mind being devious and sneaky, but a little less of the 'old' and 'dusty', if you don't mind."

"It all seemed so real," said Kaal. "I'd never have guessed that Ogun wasn't really a warlord."

"Well, I am a *great* actor," said Ray-ool Kalaam at the end of the table. "You should read the reviews of the last 4-D film I was in." He pulled out a ThinScreen and started scrolling down pages. "In fact, I think I have them here."

Seeing the looks he was getting, the actor put his ThinScreen away. "Only joking," he grinned. Dipping a spoon into his bowl of grey mush and turning to Aristil, he continued, "The food is even better than last time I was here, Aristil. Perfectly cooked Hortfish supreme with Vacheese."

"What's he talking about?" John whispered to Kaal.

"The food. Haven't you tried it yet?"

"No, it's just grey mush. Looks awful."

"Well, looks can be deceiving," Kaal answered. He nodded towards Ray-ool. "Like him. I'm still not completely certain he *isn't* an evil galactic warlord."

John dipped a spoon in the bowl and forced himself to try a mouthful of the mush. As soon as his lips closed around it, he sat up straighter, eyes wide with shock. Swallowing, he yelped, "My mum's macaroni cheese! It's my mum's macaroni cheese. But how?"

Passing behind John's chair, Socrat passed to pat him on the shoulder. "Remember. The scholars do not choose to pass on *all* their knowledge," he said, three of his eyes winking.

"Pay no attention to Socrat," said Aristil. "We call it comfort food. It's a simple invention that tells your brain that whatever food you are craving most is in your mouth. The only reason we haven't shared it with the universe is that we don't want everyone supposing that we think about our bellies all day. The Scholars of Kerallin are supposed to think about *serious* things."

"Well, this is *seriously* good," John replied heaping his spoon with comfort food.

"So, what did you think of our test?" Socrat asked the table.

"Scary," said Werril. "I haven't been so terrified since we crash-landed on Zirion Beta. Or that time we got caught up in the Subo-Goran battle on Archivus Major."

"It was painful," said Queelin, flexing her arm.

"Thinking about it, those soldier droids were pretty easy, though," said Gobi-san-Art. "I could have taken them all out on my own."

"Thanks for leaving us some, Gobi," said Lishtig. "Droid fighting was the best bit."

"I *told* you, Silva. Didn't I tell you?" wheezed Thushlar. "I could have made better droids in my lunch hour. You *always* make them too easy."

Silva looked up from a conversation he was having with Raytanna. Sunlight glittered on his metal mask. "Every year we have this argument, Thushlar," he said.

"The droids were based on the standard WarDrone model, and I'm sure Queelin didn't think they were easy to beat. If we let *you* make them, the students would never have a chance."

Soon, the whole table was laughing and arguing about whether the soldier droids had fought well.

"MY DROIDS FAILED ME," boomed Ray-ool, sounding like Ogun. "With better servants, I could have CONQUERED THE GALAXY."

"Well, I'm with Werril," said John eventually. "When I first saw Ogun, I thought my knees were going to give way. I was terrified the whole time."

"Me, too," said Emmie. "Especially when he threw Aristil against the hoverbus. Didn't that hurt?"

"I was wearing thick padding beneath my robes," said Aristil, "as Ray-ool knew." She patted the actor on the shoulder.

"The scholars acted brilliantly, too," said Kaal. "You all completely convinced me."

Mordant snorted in scorn. "Really?" he said. "I knew all along that the test was a set-up. I didn't like to say anything because the scholars had gone to so much trouble, but it was obvious."

Around the table, students giggled. John, Emmie, and Kaal looked at each other, grinning. Each of them knew exactly what the others were thinking:

Yeah, right.

CHAPTER 15

John's second bowl of comfort food had tasted like lasagne in his mouth, the third an ice cream sundae. By the time Aristil announced that it was time for the students to return to Hyperspace High, he couldn't have eaten another thing.

Goodbyes took a while. Ray-ool Kalaam returned to his ship after making every student promise, at least three times, to watch *Nebula Zone Twelve* and presenting each them each with an autographed poster. Thushlar reappeared and pressed several data chips on maths from his own collection into John's hands. Emmie and Aristil chatted and hugged several times, while Kaal and Deem talked about the latest advances in technology and Derrilian sports results.

Even Mordant Talliver found it difficult to get away from Ulara Forshart. The tiny scholar with huge spectacles seemed to have developed a fondness for the half-Gargon boy. "And how is your dear mother? I remember her very well," John heard her say. Looking embarrassed, Mordant quickly changed the subject.

Across the room, Silva and Raytanna were still swapping notes. "Once you have finished your studies on Hyperspace High, you would be welcome here as Kerallin's youngest-ever scholar," the metal-faced scholar said.

"Leave her alone, Silva," Aristil told him. "Raytanna will be welcome here in a few hundred years but I'm sure she will have more interesting things to do with her life than spend it with a lot of old fogies."

"*You* might be an old fogey, Aristil—" Silva began, his face breaking into a wide grin.

"Please, scholars," interrupted Socrat. "The day has been long. We must get the students on their way and there is a stop to make first."

"Where are we going now?" John asked Emmie

and Kaal, as they fell in together outside the canteen building.

They both shrugged.

"It seems as if we are returning to the library," said Raytanna after a while.

Lishtig groaned. "I bet the scholars want us to clear up the mess we made in there before they let us go."

"I'd forgotten about that," John replied, feeling guilty. The incredible Library of Kerallin had been completely devastated. "So many globes got broken. All that knowledge lost…"

The sentence went unfinished, as the class stepped into the library.

"Does this answer your question, John Riley?" asked Socrat, sweeping an arm out and raising several of his many eyebrows.

Droids, similar to those from Ogun's army, were hard at work – busy repairing the library. Some were restoring the fire-damaged shelves, while others were taking the globes out of their packing trays and putting them back on the shelves. Half of the library was already back to normal, with a globe glimmering in every compartment.

"All the information the globes carry is collected by a giant server deep underground," Socrat told him. "The globes themselves are easily replaced."

"In fact, we have made copies of your home worlds for each of you to take back to Hyperspace High," Aristil said. "A souvenir of your time on Kerallin and a gift from the scholars, given with our very best wishes."

John hardly knew what to say as Socrat pressed a tiny Earth globe into his hands. "This is amazing … just *awesome*," he babbled.

"Be careful how you use it," Socrat told him, seriously. "The gift is a sign of the scholars' trust in you. The globe can show you things about your planet that are hidden to most. You must choose to use that knowledge – or not use it – with wisdom."

"I–I'll do my best," said John.

"We know you will," said Aristil. "Now, it is time for you to leave. Please follow us to the hoverbus."

As they sped towards the purple pyramid for the last time, the students chattered and joked as they checked out each others' home worlds. John finally got a chance to see Emmie's parents. Peering at her globe, he saw that her mother had the same silvery hair as her daughter, cascading down her back in an ornate style. But whereas Emmie's eyes were deep navy-blue, her mother's were golden. "Wow, she's almost as beautiful as you, Emmie," he blurted, without thinking what he was saying. Feeling his face burning, he mumbled, "Ugh, I mean … that is …"

"Thanks, John," Emmie said, giggling. "This is my dad."

Grateful for the change in subject, John looked at a tall, slender Silarian with silver hair tinged slightly blue. He was standing at a podium before a roomful of beings.

"Whoa, he looks important."

"He's on the Galactic Council," Emmie said. "I wish he wasn't. It means he spends most of his time away from home."

"This is my mum," Kaal interrupted. "Look, she's feeding my little sister her first flavworms."

John peered at Kaal's globe just in time to see a baby Derrilian throwing worms into the air, her small, leathery wings beating in excitement. Kaal's mother was trying to catch them all before they hit the floor.

"Your mum looks a bit ... umm ... annoyed," said Emmie.

"Yeah, my little sister is a handful," replied Kaal. "Last time I was home she tried to eat my ThinScreen."

"And here we are," Socrat's voice broke into the conversation.

John looked up to see the shining purple pyramid before them, the sun sinking behind it. The hoverbus slowed to a stop. As the class climbed down onto the grass, John took a last look around, wondering if he would ever again set foot on Kerallin.

"You're gawping again," Kaal told him with a nudge that almost sent John sprawling.

"How many times do I have to tell you not to do that," John replied, rubbing his shoulder.

"Your knees will be pleased to hear that there is no need to pilot the pyramid all the way back to Hyperspace High, John Riley," Socrat chuckled, as he led the students inside the ship and began touching the wall. Lights and panels lit up where his fingers passed. Within a few seconds, the whole pyramid was blazing with complicated star charts and flickering numbers.

"Coordinates laid in," said the ship's computer. "Teleport in sixty seconds."

"The whole ship is going to teleport us all the way back to Hyperspace High?" Kaal gasped. "But it must be over a thousand light years away. Teleport technology isn't that advanced."

"Oh dear," said Socrat, looking over his shoulder at Aristil. "We forgot to announce our latest teleportation research."

"Yes, we must get around to that," Aristil said, shrugging. "In the meantime, students, please take your seats and strap yourselves in."

Thanking the two scholars, the class ran to the MorphSeats and obeyed the command.

"Goodbye, and good luck with your studies," said Socrat with a friendly wave. "The headmaster will have your final report within the hour."

"Send Lorem our regards," Aristil added. "Tell him we are looking forward to the day he joins us on Kerallin."

With that, the two scholars walked out into the last of the Kerallin sunshine. Behind them the pyramid wall rippled and became perfectly clear.

"Teleportation in five, four, three, two, one."

The ship seemed to spin around John. For a moment he felt as though his body had split into a million different pieces and was zipping down a long tunnel of whirling light.

The sensation lasted for less than a heartbeat.

John blinked. The pyramid was floating in space. In the distance, shining among the stars, was the elegant white shape of Hyperspace High. As always, John felt a shiver of pride run through him when he saw the great spaceship.

"Welcome back," Sergeant Jegger's voice echoed around the ship. "We'll bring you in with the force fields. Sit tight, this will take a few moments."

Lorem was at the dock to greet the returning students as they emerged from the pyramid, an Examiner floating at his side. Chattering loudly and clutching their globes, the class thronged around him.

"We passed," Emmie told him, grinning. "I made a mess of the questions, but we *passed*. I've never been so relieved in my life."

"We didn't just *pass*, we totally kicked butt. There was this warlord, headmaster, only he wasn't really a warlord, he was this actor guy, and—" Lishtig babbled.

Lorem raised a finger to his lips. "You must not speak of your adventures on Kerallin," he said. "Only say that you have been examined by the scholars and passed their tests."

"The scholars were really cool," said John. "I don't know what I was so nervous about."

"You rose to the challenge, John Riley, as I knew you all would." Looking around, the headmaster smiled. "I see that the scholars have sent you back with gifts and that tells me everything I need to know for the moment. Well done, I am proud of you all."

"Rule 274C: all students must remain in their dormitories after lights out," the Examiner droned. "Punishment for transgressions: double detention. Return to your rooms immediately."

"The Examiner is right," said Lorem with another smile. "All of you have had a long day and need rest. Plus, the scholars' report will be arriving soon, and I must admit I want to get back to my study to read it."

Still talking excitedly, the students made their way to their dormitories. After saying good night to Emmie, Kaal and John slipped into their own room.

"Good evening," said Zepp's voice, as they sank into the squashy sofas. "Can I offer you hot drinks?"

"That would be great, Zepp," sighed John. "Hot chocolate for me, please."

"Liquidized blindbeetles for me, thanks," said Kaal.

The two of them looked at each other, and then at the virtual reality helmets on the low table between them, and then back at each other again.

"Boxogle?" asked Kaal, with a grin.

"Hmmm," said John, yawning and glancing longingly at his bed pod. "It's tempting, but I think I've done enough fighting for one day."

"Ha, you're only saying that because you saw my new move on Kerallin. I am going to *crush* you."

"You think so, do you?"

Steaming mugs appeared in the drinks dispenser hatch. "The headmaster has just announced that there will be a special assembly at oh-seven-hundred-hours," said Zepp. "I strongly suggest that you sleep. In fact, if you even *look* at Boxogle, I will fry every circuit in the games console."

"You can't do that," gasped Kaal, shocked.

"*Hello* – I'm the ship's computer," said Zepp,

sounding surprisingly smug for a computer. "I can do pretty much anything I like on Hyperspace High."

"Well, that settles it," said John, yawning. "I'm going to bed."

CHAPTER 16

Early the next morning, John stood on the grass in the middle of the Centre, Emmie and Kaal on either side of him. Stars glittered beyond the great dome above. Behind him, the whole school had gathered. Dressed in the red and silver uniform of Hyperspace High, thousands of students from all over the universe lined up, waiting for the headmaster to appear on a dais that had been set up overnight. John half-turned to take a look over his shoulder. As always, he remained astonished by the variety of students who attended the school.

At the back were the largest: including the biggest

student in the school, a female Manorus called Faysha who looked a little like a two-legged tiger, if a tiger had been the size of an elephant. Next to her was a shapeshifter being who resembled a half-empty balloon in his natural state. Elsewhere in the crowd were half-droids, creatures with two heads, some with wings, and others with body parts that John couldn't begin to guess the function of.

"The headmaster's coming." Kaal nudged him, adding, "oh, sorry, I forgot," as John stumbled to one side.

John rolled his eyes and turned back to the stage, as Lorem materialized in a blaze of light.

"A very good morning to all of you," the headmaster said.

The entire school answered, "Good morning, sir," as one.

"I have some *excellent* news," Lorem continued. "The scholars of Kerallin have assessed a class of our first-year students for the first time in a century." Pausing, he looked along the rows of students before him. With a trace of a smile, he went on, "The scholars' tests can be extemely difficult, so it is with great pleasure that I tell you that our class of first years achieved an *outstanding* result."

Applause and cheers rippled through the crowd.

"And that is not all," said the headmaster. "The scholars have decided to make a special award to one student in particular. A student who showed a truly remarkable ability to apply their academic knowledge under pressure."

A hush descended. Further along the line, John heard Mordant whisper, "That will be me."

"Undoubtedly, Master Talliver, sir. The scholars of Kerallin are famous for their wisdom. They will have seen your genius," droned G-Vez, now reunited with its master.

"And that student is … *Emmie Tarz!*" Lorem announced.

Emmie gasped, as the school broke into applause again.

"There must be some mista—," Mordant Talliver began.

The rest of his sentence was quickly drowned out by cheers, as Emmie's classmates crowded around her, clapping her on the back.

"Brilliant, Emmie!" shouted John. "I *said* you were brilliant."

"Nice work, Tarz!" yelled Lishtig. "You totally deserve it."

Kaal threw his arms around her, almost crushing her slender body in a huge Derrilian hug.

"Emmie will receive an extra hundred points towards her marks for the year," said the headmaster, trying to make himself heard above the noise. "And the scholars of Kerallin have also asked me to grant the whole school a day off in recognition of her achievement."

This time, the cheers were deafening. "Emmie, Emmie, EMMIE!" chanted thousands of voices.

"So, what are you hanging around here for?" Lorem asked, laughing. "Go and enjoy yourselves!"

As the headmaster flashed away, Emmie was swamped. It seemed that everyone in the school wanted to congratulate her, though John noticed Mordant stalking away, shouting at G-Vez. Eventually, however, the crowd broke up as students went off to enjoy their unexpected day off.

Grinning, John gave his flustered friend another hug.

"So, what are we going to do with the day?" Kaal asked. "As you earned it, Emmie, you get to choose – so long as you choose Boxogle."

"No, Kaal," said John, shaking his head. "Now Emmie's an academic superstar, she'll want to spend the day studying in the library."

Emmie punched him on the arm. "Idiot human," she giggled. "No library, no Boxogle. With all that water yesterday, I just remembered how long it's been since I visited the SwimBubble."

"What's a SwimBubble?" John asked.

Emmie and Kaal stopped and looked at each other in a way that John had come to recognize – pity mixed with wonder.

"He's never been in a SwimBubble, Kaal," said Emmie in hushed tones.

Kaal shook his head sadly. "Sometimes I wonder if they have any fun at all on Earth, Emmie," he said.

"Yes, but what's a SwimBubble?" John repeated, exasperated.

Both of his friends ignored him. "Hey, Lishtig!" Kaal shouted. "The Earthling's never seen a SwimBubble!"

"What are we waiting for, then?" Lishtig called

back. "I'll round everyone up."

Half an hour later, wearing red and silver trunks that Zepp had provided, John stepped out of the changing rooms with Emmie and Kaal on either side of him.

"*This* is a SwimBubble," said Emmie.

John goggled, his jaw hanging open. *Really freaky space stuff*, he thought, not for the first time.

Before him was a vast room with a ceiling that looked out onto space. John hardly noticed the view, his eyes fixed on what the huge space contained. Its surface rippling gently, what looked like a globe made completely of water hung in zero-gravity. Reflected light shimmered on the white walls.

"B-but that's im-*impossible*," he stuttered, gazing up at the vast blue ball.

"Not impossible, just beyond your planet's technology," said Kaal.

"Stop standing about gawping!" shouted Lishtig, pushing past. "Last one in's a loser." Kicking off as he entered the zero-gravity room, the purple-haired boy dived up into the water, making waves that spread out across the surface of the globe.

"Off you go, then," said Kaal. From behind, John felt the Derrilian give him a powerful push, sending him flying upward. He splashed into the giant water ball in a tangle of arms and legs.

"Dive bomb!" shrieked Kaal.

John almost choked with water and laughter as the Derrilian plunged in beside him. One after another, his classmates followed, their shrieks and laughs echoing off the walls. Gulping a breath, John dived under, following his classmate, Queelin, as she darted gracefully through the SwimBubble. He came out near the top, looking up in amazement at the stars speeding past outside Hyperspace High as he trod water.

Kaal surfaced next to him; Emmie's head appeared a second later. "So what do you think, Earthling?" she asked, pushing wet hair out of her eyes.

John lay back, allowing himself to float on top of the rippling ball, looking out into the darkness as Hyperspace High swept past a gas giant planet.

"I think," he said eventually, "that I totally *love* this school."

Here's a sneak preview of the next
Hyperspace High adventure…

GALACTIC BATTLE

CHAPTER 1

John Riley's shared dorm was like a plush hotel room, with luxurious sofas and vast enclosed beds. And the floor-to-ceiling window had a view that no hotel on Earth could have matched. But as John gazed out at black outer space twinkling with stars, he couldn't help wishing instead for a view of trees and grass. He longed to see a clear blue sky with fluffy white clouds. It had been several weeks since he'd left Earth, and he was feeling a bit homesick for his world. John let out a deep sigh.

"What's wrong, John?" his room-mate Kaal asked.

"Oh, nothing," John replied, forcing a smile. "Just

missing home a bit."

"I know exactly how you feel," Kaal said sympathetically. "I can't wait to see my folks at the Space Specta—" Kaal cut himself off abruptly, before continuing awkwardly. "Sorry, John. I keep forgetting that your parents can't come."

A gloomy silence descended over their room. But it was soon broken by the sound of an incoming video call. Suddenly, three demonic, green-skinned figures filled one of the two video screens on the desk. They leaned in close, their wings rustling behind them, and grinned, revealing white, shark-like teeth.

Kaal, who looked exactly like the aliens on the screen, grinned back at them and waved happily. "Hi, Mum! Hi, Dad! It's so good to see you! How's little Varka? Hi, Kulvi. Hey, you've had your teeth sharpened! Nice!"

"You're looking well, son," rumbled the largest alien, who John guessed was Kaal's father. "Varka is sleeping, thank goodness. She's finally had her first skin-shedding— Ah, I didn't realize your room-mate was there, too! Hello, John."

John, who was sprawled on one of the sofas, looked

up from his holocomic. "Wide skies, Mr Tartaru," he said, giving the traditional Derrilian greeting Kaal had taught him. Even though Kaal and his family were speaking their native language, John could understand every word they were saying, thanks to Hyperspace High's computer system, which translated everything into the language of each individual listener.

"And good flight to you, too, young man!" Kaal's father responded, clearly impressed.

"What excellent manners your friend has," said Kaal's mother.

"Wonder where he learned them?" Kulvi said, with warmth and wickedness in her voice. "Surely not from my little brother Kaal. You want to watch out for him, John; he's a savage. Hey, Kaal. Remember when you put the scutterliches in my bed?"

"They needed somewhere warm to hatch or they'd have died!" Kaal protested.

John tried not to laugh. He'd heard Kaal's side of this story a hundred times.

"Now, Kaal," his mother said, "this chit-chat is very pleasant, but we must discuss our visit to Hyperspace High. There are only three days to go."

"I know," Kaal said, fidgeting with excitement. "I can't wait!"

"We're looking forward to it too, dear one. But there are arrangements to make! Did you reserve a docking space for the family starhopper? We won't be the only family coming to visit! And where are we going to sit during the Space Spectacular? You can't leave these things to the last minute, you know."

John grinned and retreated behind his holocomic, leaving Kaal to chat excitedly to his family.

It was funny how mums and dads were much the same all over the galaxy, if Kaal's were anything to go by. His own mother would have been just as fussy about the arrangements. John idly wondered what his mum and dad would make of Kaal's family. They'd probably run screaming ... like John nearly had, the first day he'd met Kaal.

"Hey, do you know if the Tarz family is coming?" Kulvi said. "I haven't seen Brannicus Tarz in years! He's a bigwig on the Galactic Council now."

"Of course they are!" Kaal said. "This *is* the Space Spectacular we're talking about. Everyone's family is coming!" Then he stopped in his tracks. "Um. Almost everyone's, I mean. Not all the families can make it, of course."

"Of course," his father echoed. There was another awkward silence.

John winced. Neither Kaal nor his family had looked in John's direction, but he knew they were talking about him. He was the only student on Hyperspace High whose parents would never – *could* never – visit the school.

It wasn't just the distance. Unlike all the other parents, John's mum and dad didn't even know he was here on Hyperspace High. They thought he was at a boarding school back on Earth. All those weeks ago, John had accidentally climbed aboard a space shuttle that he'd thought was the coach taking him to his new boarding school in Derbyshire. Instead, he was taken far away into the galaxy, to the best space school in the universe: Hyperspace High. John, the first Earthling to ever board the school, had almost been being expelled seconds after arriving – here, that meant being thrown out of an airlock! It was only thanks to the intervention of Lorem, the school's headmaster, that John had been allowed to stay on as a pupil.

So far, John had managed to keep his parents thinking that he was at the Earth boarding school. There had been a few narrow escapes, though, like the time he'd had to pretend an alien in his room was a science project. That had been a close shave …

"Do you two even know what you're doing for the Spectacular?" Kulvi asked.

"We haven't even been assigned to our groups yet," Kaal said. "That's happening at twelve sharp today, in the Centre. I might get Galactic Battle, Plasma Sculpting, Zero-G Acrobatics – even Star Dance! Can you imagine me dancing?"

Read
GALACTIC BATTLE
to find out what happens next!

For more exciting books from brilliant
authors, follow the fox!
www.curious-fox.com